# UNCONDITIONAL

## A STORY OF FATHERHOOD, LOST LOVE, AND LIFELONG FRIENDSHIP

## STEPHEN KOGON

www.stephenkogon.com

Cover design by: Ann Weinstock
Interior design by: Michael Grossman

ISBN: 979-8-9989750-2-8 (hardcover)
ISBN: 979-8-9989750-1-1 (paperback)
ISBN: 979-8-9989750-0-4 (ebook)

*For my mother, Janette Kogon,*
*who loves books more than anyone I know.*

# PART 1

# CHAPTER 1

"My friends, after sixteen years in the NFL, our guy Kenny is hanging it up," Matthew Russell stated somberly, standing next to his two best friends, Kenny and Sherry Mitchell, inside Phoenix's oldest karaoke bar, Pibbs, as onlooking friends held up their beer bottles.

Sherry, the same age as Matthew at thirty-five, nodded in appreciation as her husband Kenny, thirty-seven, held his head up proudly.

The three of them had met in college, the University of Arizona, at a party one of Kenny's football teammates was hosting in an off-campus apartment. Kenny was the star running back of the team, and with his gregarious personality, parties he went to were usually well-attended.

Kenny and Sherry weren't a couple yet, just friends, although it was obvious to Matthew where things were heading.

"It's not that these young bucks have passed him by with their superior speed and athleticism," Matthew continued. "It's that their all-encompassing inferiority has finally bored him to where he just couldn't take it anymore."

"That's right!" Kenny bellowed. "And don't ya'll forget it."

Sherry held up her glass of water, which stood out among the sea of bottles. "When you're just too good for the room, you gotta get up and leave the room," she said.

"My baby spittin' the truth," Kenny said, smiling with a nod.

"Let's drink to that," Sherry said.

Everyone in their area drank their beer. Pibbs was a beer and shots bar. All the drinkers in their area had either a Bud Light, a Heineken, or a Corona. Matthew went with a Heineken, instead of his usual Bud Light. It was a celebration after all, he said to himself chuckling when he ordered it.

Matthew knew most of the people in their party as they were his friends, too, with some being co-workers for the Arizona Cardinals football team, in which he was a team photographer. The same team Kenny was retiring from.

Then Sherry held up her glass again. "And now he's coming home full-time so we can tackle that miles-long chores list he said he didn't have time for 'cause of football."

"Here, here!" Matthew said with a smile.

"I didn't like that toast as much," Kenny retorted.

Matthew raised his Heineken, "And I can take pics of other players doing amazing things without getting a text that says, 'I thought we were friends.'"

Everyone chuckled and took a drink as Larry, Matthew's boss—who ran the Cardinals media department—gave a hearty "Here, here."

"These toasts are getting worse," Kenny said, clearly enjoying the ribbing as he shook his head while smiling.

Matthew and Kenny's life and careers ran on a similar track, as before his job with the Cardinals, Matthew was a sports photographer for the University of Arizona's newspaper, The Daily Wildcat. That's when he began taking pictures of Kenny's exploits on the football field.

And Kenny accomplished the rare feat of playing his whole career, sixteen years, in one state due to being drafted by the Arizona Cardinals. A total anomaly as most running backs only lasted five to ten years, and often ended up playing for several different teams.

"And now it's time for the man of the hour to speak," Matthew said, looking at Kenny proudly. Everyone in their area cheered loudly and held up their drink.

Kenny held up his Corona. "Guys, you know I love this game. But it's time." He nodded with a tinge of sadness. "I apparently have chores in my future—and I'll be extra busy never sending any texts to my so-called photographer friend who cheats on our friendship by hyping up others."

"Worst toast ever," Matthew said, laughing along with the crowd.

"Here, here," Sherry said through her laughter.

They all drank. Kenny took a moment. The crowd fell silent, and Kenny swallowed hard. Matthew thought he saw a slight tear in his eye. Then Kenny took a deep breath and pasted his smile back on, holding his drink aloft.

"But seriously, ya'll. Thanks for sending me off. Don't know exactly what the future holds—but having everyone here in my life is gonna make whatever comes next okay."

Everyone smiled, and one by one, each in their group gave Kenny a hearty hug.

Matthew hugged him last while saying, "You did your thing, my friend. And it was an honor to witness it all."

"Luv ya, brother," Kenny said, dapping Matthew up after the hug. "Now let's karaoke it up, ya'll. This is a celebration."

Kenny walked with a tiny limp over to the slightly elevated stage, the centerpiece of the room. Everyone in their group followed.

Grabbing the mic off the stand like it belonged in his hand, Kenny bobbed up and down as the beat to Bobby Brown's "My Prerogative" began playing.

He glanced at the small monitor displaying the lyrics, and belted out the song to cheers and laughter. A multi-colored spotlight washed over the stage as he moved around with a dramatic flair, adding in his best attempt at an old-school Bobby Brown dance move.

Before he could get too deep into his thoughts, Sherry nudged him. "He's done this song a million times. I keep telling him to vary it."

"The man knows what he likes," Matthew said. He looked down at her plastic cup of water. "C'mon, you gotta have a real drink. It's his retirement party."

"Busy day tomorrow, bub."

Sherry had spent the years after graduating college with a business degree rising in the ranks of a commercial agency, eventually becoming a VP—but it was no surprise when she changed gears to start her own speaking agency last year.

"Ya'll take care of the bottle, I'll take care of the business," Matthew said, imitating her voice, and waving his finger around the way she did when she said it.

"I stand by it. Who's the one organizing all our parties?"

"I think you could enjoy a Fuzzy Navel and still organize a party."

"Fuzzy Navel? No bartender here has ever made one of them. And I haven't had one since I was 19."

"It's all I could think of in the moment. And it could be your drink. The orange juice makes it healthy."

"Weirdo," she said laughing at him. Then, as if remembering something, she said with a wry smile, "Guess who's coming by soon?"

"You didn't invite your realtor friend, did you?" he asked. She was always trying to set him up. He knew she genuinely wanted to see him happy, but she also really enjoyed playing matchmaker.

"I wouldn't spring her on you like that," Sherry said. "Well, I would. I didn't think of it. No, it's Monica. She's back in town."

Matthew's face slightly flushed as Sherry chuckled.

"Don't even try playing it off," she said, still chuckling.

Matthew's mouth went a little dry. Sherry knew him too well. "It's been three years," he said wistfully.

Sherry laughed. "Is that marked on your calendar?"

Matthew could only chuckle slightly. Monica was the only girl he dated that he ever truly liked. Before her, he had a rep for being a serial dater, and for being too picky.

He and Monica first met as sophomores in Sherry's dorm when she had a small gathering of friends. Monica lived on the same floor, and she and Sherry became quick friends. She thought Matthew and Monica would hit it off—and she was right. It was instant. Not just the mutual attraction, but they liked each other's personalities and started dating almost immediately.

"I wonder why she didn't tell me," Matthew said. "Is it a pop-in visit?"

"Don't know," Sherry answered. "And she didn't want it to be a surprise 'cause she told me to tell you."

"We haven't talked in a minute."

"You still make each other a little nervous. That's probably why she didn't tell you."

When he and Monica first started dating, they never talked too specifically about the future. He knew he wanted to be a photographer, preferably in sports. And she, as an anthropology major, was fascinated by the world. He loved listening to her talk about world history, cultures, and art. She was much more cultured than him, but they embraced their differences; both taking pleasure in listening to whatever the other was passionate about.

But she didn't know what she wanted from life until their senior year when her aspirations crystallized into traveling to every country on earth that was safe, and to get paid chronicling her journeys. How she'd light up whenever she talked about it.

But Matthew had no interest in that life, especially right out of college. He wanted to stay in Arizona and get his dream job, the one he currently had with the Cardinals.

They had many conversations about how to make things work, until they finally had to conclude their differing life priorities would be too much to overcome. It saddened them because so much about their being together was fantastic. They parted amicably and stayed in touch periodically.

After their breakup and graduation, she immediately left for her first adventure, Thailand, where she got a job at the U.S. Embassy and stayed for eight months.

It was hard dating after her. No one made him feel like she did. And while he felt he made the right choice, he couldn't fight the feeling that she may have been the one that got away.

Kenny pointed to Sherry from the stage. "You're next, baby," he said, his voice echoing in the fake reverb of the microphone.

As Sherry sauntered to the stage, she turned to Matthew and said, "It's okay to smile."

He fought a smile, and she said, "Uh huh."

Sherry climbed on stage and Kenny handed her the mic. "Time for the showstopper!" Sherry bellowed, and the crowd cheered from the dance floor. Tina Turner's "You Better Be Good To Me," came on and Sherry sang and pranced, full of energy. The crowd of twelve closest to the stage bounced and swayed with her.

Matthew hung back and sipped his Heineken, in thought. Monica visiting led him back to the moment he was having. It wasn't actually a sudden moment, more like a years-long running dialogue with himself about where his own life was going. And it was a confusing dialogue, because there was so much about his life that he loved. Still, something felt like it was missing.

His friends assumed it was because he didn't have a partner. While that would make sense, deep down he wasn't sure it was accurate. He dated periodically and believed he'd welcome a partner if he found the right person. But he didn't crave companionship. He wanted it, he just didn't crave it. Too many times when he'd tell people that they'd counter with, "But people were meant to be together." And he'd counter with, "But a lot of those people force being together, and then regret it. It has to be right."

During Monica's last visit three years ago, they did try again. He spent as much of his non-work time traveling with her, and she spent time in Arizona with him when he had to work. But they both agreed the arrangement felt forced, and they, again, wouldn't be able to make it work. The only way it could have worked was if he had left his job and become a free-lance photographer, as he had done when he first started out. That would mean picking up gigs wherever he happened to be in the world.

He didn't want to do that, though, and so the rekindling attempt ended.

But when she left, he kept himself up at night wondering if he'd made the right decision.

As he reminisced, he saw Monica walk into the bar, as if on cue. Her black hair was now in a bob, but she still had that same confident, carefree way about her. And, to him, she was just as pretty as ever.

They made eye contact and smiled. Matthew felt a jolt go right through him. She walked over and they hugged. He missed hugging her. Her hair smelled like lavender, which he remembered was her favorite scent. The hug lingered a little, enough to make him think she missed hugging him, too.

Upon separating, she said, "I'd make an 'Of all the gin joints in the world' joke, but this is where you always seem to go."

"If I hopped the world like you, bartenders wouldn't know my favorite drink," Matthew replied.

"Is that favorite drink—any beer?" she said.

They smiled again as they looked each other over. She was wearing black high-wasted jeans and a purple satin blouse. The jeans were tucked into jaguar-designed ankle boots.

"Stylish as ever," he said.

"Are those the same belt and slacks I helped you buy?"

"No," he said. "Maybe. Probably."

They both laughed.

"You still look five-nine," she said. "I'm waiting for you to shrink so I can be taller."

"I don't think people shrink three inches."

"How about you shrink an inch and a half and I'll only wear heels," she said with a smile as she poked him in the stomach playfully.

"Done," he said. They both smiled, but neither had follow-up banter so they stood in silence for a moment.

Finally, he asked, "How long you back for?"

"I've got a week off."

He nodded. Sherry finished the Tina Turner song to cheers and then pointed to a man by the song control booth and said, "Ron, I'm going again. Cue up that one I told you I'd do."

Beyonce's "Single Ladies" started playing and Sherry pointed at Monica, who laughed.

"It's almost as if we're personal to her," Monica said.

"Her matchmaking rep is on the line," Matthew said, chuckling.

They both started doing Beyonce's hand dance move back at Sherry, singing along to, "*If you liked it you shoulda' put a ring on it.*"

Sherry stifled a laugh as Kenny and a few others danced over to join Matthew and Monica in the Beyonce sing-along.

The karaoke ended with Sherry, and Rihanna's "Love on the Brain" came over the sound system, so couples started slow dancing, including Sherry and Kenny.

Matthew and Monica looked at each other, as if saying, "Should we dance?" and then he held out his hand. She smiled and accepted.

They had slow danced often before, but since it had been a few years, it started a little awkwardly as he wasn't sure where to place his hands. After a few indecisive moments, he put his hands on her waist, and she put her arms around his neck.

The first thirty seconds they swayed, looking at each other, almost shy-like, but as he got more comfortable, they moved closer until finally resting cheek to cheek.

It instantly brought back all the memories of dancing with her before. Her cheek against his felt so soft. And he could really smell the lavender in her hair now, intoxicated by it with every breath he took.

The song ended, and a new slow song came on, one Matthew didn't recognize. Monica whispered in his ear, "Wanna get out of here?"

Matthew looked over at Kenny, who was still slow dancing with Sherry. Kenny smiled and nodded, as if saying it was okay for Matthew to leave the party. He nodded back, then walked out hand in hand with Monica.

The parking lot was well-lit as the moon was nearly full. Matthew and Monica walked towards his car.

"Still driving the Audi, huh?" she said.

"Uh, Audi A5, thank you very much."

"I see you're still ridiculous about your car," she teased.

"Uh, that would be very ridiculous. Thank you very much."

They got in. "You in the mood for the night air?" he asked.

"Always," she replied.

He nodded and brought the car top down, then drove off. The night air in mid-February felt crisp, like in the mid-50s.

Traffic was light, which allowed him to drive without any stop-and-go. He loved the feel of the wind on his face, especially on a crisp night.

After twenty minutes on the road, he pulled into Tempe Beach Park's near-empty parking lot.

"Was this where we went on our fourth date?" she asked.

"Good memory," he answered.

"You weren't driving an Audi then. Sorry, Audi 5."

"I had the black Dodge Charger. You didn't like how loud it was."

"Ah, yes. I remember now. It was obnoxiously loud."

"It purred like a kitten." And then they said at the same time, "A kitten on steroids."

They both laughed as they got out of the car. "I can still finish your sentences," she said.

"I hope that's on your resume."

"First line."

They laughed again and walked towards the benches overlooking the water, sitting on one. There were a few people walking the pedestrian path about fifty yards away, but no one else was around.

Their bench overlooked the water, which glistened as the moon's soft light reflected off the surface, creating tiny sparkles that danced with each ripple.

"I've missed this," Matthew said, cuddling her.

"Me too," Monica replied.

They stayed quiet for several moments, the unspoken topic hanging heavy between them. Finally, he couldn't take it any longer. "How long 'til your lease in Spain is up?" he asked hesitantly, wary of ruining the moment.

"Two months."

"And then?"

She didn't answer.

"Antarctica?" he said with a smile.

She laughed. "I can handle some cold, but not that... I do like the penguins, though."

They sat in more silence before she finally said, "I have an offer for Peru."

He understood. Arizona was still not her destination of choice.

"Amazing things to photograph there," she said hopefully.

He laughed. "I don't know if anything beats football."

"You've been with the team, what, five years?

"Nearing ten."

She knew from her visit three years ago that his job was nearly year-round. She was initially baffled by it since the games were only played from September through mid-February, and only that long if your team made the playoffs and Super Bowl. But football rarely slept. After a month off, new players joined the team via free agency in March, and then the rookie draft in April, then periods of practices through June until another month off. Then training camp in late July, preseason games in August, and then a new season started. Someone had to be there to take all the pictures.

"Could you be happy shooting something other than sports?"

"I think I could. I mean I love photography, so, yeah."

More silence. He finally said, "Does Phoenix pull you in even a tinier bit more than it used to?"

"Yes… No… Sometimes… All of the above."

He smiled, realizing she was just as indecisive as him.

"We couldn't see sometimes here, sometimes elsewhere working last time," he said.

"That was last time," she said with the same hopeful inflection.

They kept cuddling in silence. This was one of those forks in the road. While he couldn't imagine changing his life, he really enjoyed having her in his arms.

But making decisions was always difficult for him. Big ones, obviously, but even little ones. Kenny had nicknamed him "Mr. Indecisive" long ago after a restaurant outing where the server had to keep coming back because Matthew couldn't decide between the Pasta Primavera and Spaghetti Bolognese. They both sounded delicious. But the nickname had been a running joke ever since. He waffled for six months before finally buying a home. He took over two months to settle on his Audi.

But this decision, altering a life he enjoyed for the potential of an even more enjoyable life was especially tough. There was like a fog in his brain that made it difficult to even think clearly about it.

Monica knew this about him. "Let's enjoy the week together and then see where we're at," she said.

"You're only able to stay the week?"

"Yeah, I'm on a bookkeeping gig this time. Not my favorite, and I don't get paid for time off."

"What about your travel articles?"

"I don't make as much off them as I used to. The market is kind of saturated."

"Okay, let's Monica-Matthew the week up."

"So romantic when you put it that way," she said laughing.

"Casanova strikes again," he retorted, when his phone rang, snapping them out of the moment.

He went to turn his ringer off when he saw the caller's area code was New Mexico.

"New Mexico. It's where my brother lives. But this isn't his number." He looked at her.

"You should probably answer," she said.

He nodded and answered.

"Hello," Matthew said.

"Hello, is this Matthew Russell?" the caller asked.

"Yes," Matthew replied.

"This is Jeff Turner with the Albuquerque Police Department. I'm afraid I have some bad news. Your brother Paul has passed away."

Matthew's jaw dropped, stunned. Monica saw and grabbed his hand.

"What?" was the only thing Matthew could muster saying.

"He and a woman he was with, we're assuming his wife or partner, took their lives. I'm very sorry."

Matthew couldn't make sense of his thoughts. He blurted out, "Are you sure?"

"Yes. They plugged up their car's exhaust pipe and sat in their car in their garage until … it happened."

"Did they leave a note?"

"Yes. It said, 'Please take care of our baby.'"

"A baby?" Matthew exclaimed.

"A three-day-old girl. We tracked her down. She's still in the hospital. A preemie. When was the last time you spoke with your brother?"

Matthew paused. It'd been over a year since he and Paul spoke. Paul was three years older, and they had a difficult relationship. When they were kids they got along pretty well, then had up and down times during the teen years, then went back to getting along okay in their early 20s.

But as Paul got older, he started having major problems with depression, and it often manifested itself in anger. He would go on long rants, and Matthew put up with it for years before finally deciding he didn't want to listen to the ranting anymore.

The last time they spoke, Paul ranted about how Matthew wasn't friendly to his girlfriend, Kim, which had been bizarre to Matthew because he had only met Kim once—and felt it was just an awkward encounter. She had social anxiety and couldn't really hold a conversation or even look him in the eye. So, they sat in uncomfortable silence before Matthew finally excused himself.

Kim and Paul had interpreted that as being unfriendly. Matthew would have apologized if she misconstrued things that way, but Paul just started ranting, so Matthew hung up. They hadn't spoken since.

It bothered him from time to time that his only remaining family member was not a part of his life at all, but he wasn't in a hurry to remedy it. He mostly never thought about it because Paul was out of sight, out of mind. He figured that maybe one day they'd reconcile, but who knew when?

"Not in a little while," Matthew finally answered, muted. "What happens next?"

"Social services will deal with the baby. I can text their info."

"Yes, please do."

"I'm sorry again for your loss."

"Thank you," Matthew said. He hung up and looked at Monica.

"My brother."

She nodded, understanding. He slumped down, the reality of what happened hitting him more. Monica rubbed his arm.

"I'm going to have to go to New Mexico."

"Of course," she said.

"I'm sorry."

"No, no, don't be. We'll deal with us down the line. You take care of what you need to."

He nodded thanks. "I better start making my plans."

She nodded and they left, driving off in silence until they arrived at her hotel. He parked out front.

"Are you going to be okay?" Monica asked.

"My mind's a mess right now."

She gave him a small reassuring smile and they hugged.

"We'll talk soon," he said.

He watched her walk to her hotel room. She turned around and waved goodbye. He waved back. When she was safely inside, he drove off. His mind was a mess. While stopped at a light he received a text from the police officer that said, *Here's the social worker to contact.*

Matthew called the number. A woman answered.

"Hi, I was given this number to call about my brother Paul Russell's baby."

"Yes, hi, I was expecting your call," the social worker responded.

"I'm at a complete loss," Matthew said. "Paul and I were kind of estranged, so I know nothing about the situation. Except that she's a preemie."

"I'm learning myself, so I don't have a lot of information right now. They named her Allie."

"Okay. What happens with a baby in this situation?"

"A lot of that will depend on how you want to handle things."

"I don't think I'm the one who'll handle things. Have you reached Kim's, the mother's, family?"

"I did. Her parents said they disowned her over twenty years ago and hadn't been in touch since." She paused awkwardly, then continued, "And they wanted nothing to do with the baby."

"What?" Matthew said, stunned. "They know she has no parents now?"

"Trust me, it was not a good conversation."

Matthew could hear the tiredness in her voice.

"They kept repeating that Kim was a sinner, and to them she was dead a long time ago. I kept saying, 'But the baby's not Kim,' and they repeated they wanted nothing to do with her and that Paul's family could handle it. And they asked not to be contacted again."

Matthew exhaled audibly. He could not believe how things were unraveling. The decision regarding the future of this 3-day-old girl, an orphan, a decision that would affect the rest of her life, was going to fall entirely on him, "Mr. Indecisive."

# CHAPTER 2

"Allie's a pretty name," Sherry said.

"Yeah," Matthew replied, his mind swirling. He was packing a small suitcase in his bedroom: a pair of jeans, three pairs of slacks, underwear, socks, two dress shirts, two plain white T-shirts, a sports coat and two ties.

He was heading to New Mexico to settle Paul's affairs, and then explore all the options for the newborn.

The room was simple and mostly neat, except for a pair of sweatpants strewn over a chair. A queen-sized bed sat against one wall, flanked by a nightstand with a lamp, a book about finance, a notepad with a list of to-dos: 1) buy avocados, 2) oil change, 3) get navy jacket dry cleaned. A desk in a corner had a desktop with the Arizona Cardinals logo as a screensaver.

Kenny tapped the plastic face shield of the helmet. "Is this a Patrick Mahomes helmet?"

Matthew nodded as he tried to figure out if he had enough clothing. He hadn't picked a return date but assumed he'd only be there a few days to a week. He was probably overpacking, but he had no idea.

"You display his and not one of mine?" Kenny asked.

"He's Patrick Mahomes," Matthew answered.

"Mmm," Kenny muttered, sounding a little jealous. Then shrugged, "All right, can't hate on that." He returned his focus to Matthew. "When was the last time you talked with Paul?"

"Been a year at least," Matthew answered, shaking his head at the absurdity of it all.

Sherry also shook her head. "How can you have a baby and do that to yourself?" she asked. "And for both of them to do it. To be that troubled." She sighed.

"Some folks don't want to be in this world anymore," Kenny said. Then he asked, "Did you know the wife—or girlfriend, whatever she was?"

"Not really," Matthew replied. "I knew she had similar mental issues."

"Do you have any idea what you're going to do?" Sherry asked.

Matthew knew they were both thinking about his indecisiveness. How could they not? He answered her with just a small chuckle and a shrug. She gave him a hug.

"You want me to come with you?" Kenny asked.

"No. I gotta deal with this alone," he answered.

His flight was in four hours, and Kenny would drive him to the airport. Monica would be here any minute to say goodbye. He didn't know if he'd be back in Arizona before she had to head back to Spain.

Kenny and Sherry said goodbye, and Sherry told him to call if he needed to chat. Kenny told him to text when he was ready to be picked up and Matthew said he'd be ready in a little over an hour.

"That's awfully early," Kenny said.

"I prefer early," Matthew replied.

His home in Gilbert was only twenty-five minutes from the Phoenix airport, but he once almost missed a flight due to an accident on the US-60 W.

As Kenny and Sherry left, Matthew put his suitcase by the door and began staring at the Patrick Mahomes helmet when Monica walked in, subdued.

"Hey," she said. "Sherry and Kenny let me in."

"Hey," he said back, still standing by his collectibles.

"That have significance?" she asked, motioning to the helmet.

"The last good conversation I had with Paul was about this. Only thing we ever had in common was loving football."

He turned to her. They managed small smiles.

"This kind of shakes things up with us," he said.

"We can deal with us later," she replied.

"I don't know how long I'll be in New Mexico."

"Get everything sorted out and then we can … have our talk."

He nodded. And he really wanted to keep his mind off his ordeal so he insisted she tell him stories of her travels, even though he'd heard a bunch already. She indulged, leaning into the ones he'd previously had the most interest in—her mountain climbing. She started with her most recent trek up Jebel Saghro Circuit in south-east Morocco and how it was one of the best for off-the-beaten-track trekking.

As she finished detailing the types of rock formations and canyons she saw, he started wondering why he'd never mountain climbed.

"You're looking wistful," she said.

"Just started thinking about things I've never done before."

"You're still young."

He chuckled because he usually didn't have thoughts like this. He never felt like he was in a rut, so there was never an urgency to do things outside of his daily routine.

"You've also just had a major 'life is fleeting' moment. That usually makes one think."

She was right. And he hadn't had a lot of 'life is fleeting' moments. The last was when each of his parents passed. His father went first, of a heart attack when Matthew was a teenager. It happened the day before they were supposed to go to a Cardinals game, the first home game that season. The suddenness was so shocking. The night before, his father, Paul and him were jumping around the living room chanting,

"Card-in-als," which they always giddily did in the days leading up to a game they'd be attending.

After that, Paul had a harder time being a Cardinals fan, but Matthew's love for them never waned. He and his father were diehard fans—the thing that bonded them the most—and so staying a diehard fan felt right, as if his father would have been mad if he had abandoned them.

His mother, who he was extremely close to, died of breast cancer five years ago. It hit hard. Very hard. He was the person he was because of her. They had similar personalities, even similar sense of humors—but it was how she treated people that left the biggest mark on him. She was kind and caring and made everyone feel better. Nearly everyone at her funeral said the same thing, "Your mom was such a lovely person."

And both his parents would have been so devastated by Paul taking his own life. In a way, he was glad they weren't around to feel that pain.

Monica told a few more stories; the last one before he had to head to the airport was about her attempt to climb Mt. Everest, which she had to abort due to an illness.

Kenny was on his way to pick Matthew up, and Monica had arranged for an Uber. As it arrived, they shared a long hug and a quick kiss. He still didn't know whether his future would be with her. And he couldn't even wrap his head around it. It'd have to all wait until he resolved everything in New Mexico.

As Monica's Uber drove away, Kenny's Mustang GT pulled up. Matthew put his suitcase in the trunk, and they left, sitting in silence at first. But Kenny wasn't a silence guy. They stayed away from what Matthew would do, so the focus landed on Kenny talking about being a speaker, which meant being one of Sherry's clients. He laughed, saying he would probably drive her crazy. Matthew agreed, as he was a serial ad-libber.

Kenny dropped him off at the airport with a big hug and a, "You got this, brother."

Boarding was fairly fast, and Matthew stared out the window as the plane took off for New Mexico. Then a baby started crying. He'd heard plenty of crying babies on planes before, but this one jolted him, being reminded that he had a newborn's future in his hands. He looked over. The child's mother was bouncing the baby and rocking back and forth, shushing and trying to insert a pacifier, looking apologetic. She caught his eye and mouthed, "I'm sorry."

He nodded to her that it was okay, then went back to looking out the window. He thought about babies.

They were kind of foreign to him. He'd never had a younger sibling or cousins or anything. His only experience was Kenny and Sherry's kids, and he never helped take care of them.

He knew babies ate baby food but didn't know what that comprised or how often they ate. When did they start eating actual food? How often did they need their diapers changed, or when did they stop wearing diapers? Even though he had no reason to know any of these things, he still felt a little odd that he was so clueless.

And he still didn't know what decision he would make about the little girl. She was his niece, but he felt odd thinking of her that way. They had no connection whatsoever. He had looked up information about orphanages and foster care, but it all felt impersonal and foreign. These things existed, though, so he knew it wasn't abnormal for a child to grow up in them.

But how deeply would he pursue options for her? If he toured facilities, what would he even be looking for? Would he just go with his gut? The whole idea of it was so strange, handing a little human off to strangers. But the little human was also a stranger.

He felt horrible for her, though. That her parents would just leave her alone and helpless. The more he thought about it, the more the fog in his head swirled. He couldn't concentrate. He'd have to decide at some point, but until that point arrived, he would try not to overthink it.

He'd also have plenty on his plate concerning Paul, making all kinds of decisions about his affairs. For all he knew, he might also need to make decisions about Kim, even though he only met her the one time. It was too much. He closed his eyes and leaned back, letting the clouds overtake his mind so he could sleep.

He awoke just as the plane made its descent into Albuquerque International Sunport. He'd never flown into this airport before. The desert landscapes were stunning. And he was pretty sure the river winding through a valley was the Rio Grande. To make the view even more spectacular, they arrived at sunset, with fiery orange and red streaks stretching across the horizon.

Being welcomed by such beauty and sadness made his breath catch in his throat. Life unfolded in such unusual ways. And this trip to New Mexico might be the most unusual thing of all.

# CHAPTER 3

Matthew's first stop was Paul's apartment in Deming, New Mexico. He stood in the cluttered and unkempt main room with the building's apartment manager, Stan, whose permanent frown made clear he didn't want to be dealing with this.

Only two things were on the walls, paintings that Matthew guessed were each surrealist. One was of a parrot's head on top of forest animals: a rabbit, squirrel and chipmunk. The other a mishmash of psychedelic colors. Looking at each caused a little eye strain for Matthew—and it was another difference between him and Paul. He preferred realism.

There were two bedrooms, a kitchen, a bathroom and a main room. Everything needed a thorough cleaning. Mounds of cluttered junk and old stained furniture would also need to be removed. Was it his responsibility? He didn't see why it would be, but he also felt guilty about whoever had to deal with it.

Neither Paul nor Kim left any kind of will.

"The last six months they were always behind on the rent," Stan said. "Your brother told me they'd both been unemployed for months and had lots of debt."

Matthew knew Paul was a landscaper who worked on a gig-to-gig basis. At least that's what he did before they stopped talking. The last year in Paul's life was now a guessing game.

Did the work become too hard on his body? Did depression overwhelm and incapacitate him? He knew questions like that, and many others, would probably never get answered.

Matthew also imagined their financial situation probably played some part in their decision. Had Paul ever considered coming to him for financial help? Not that Matthew could be that helpful. On his salary he was able to pay his bills and save some, but he wasn't rolling in money.

If Paul had considered coming to him, it was probably short-lived, as he was way too proud to come to his younger brother for money. Or maybe he was still too angry about his interaction with Kim.

Matthew shook his head and wished Paul had just had a rational conversation with him instead of yelling as soon as they started talking. He could have explained that he in no way meant to be unfriendly to Kim. He just didn't know how to act around her.

And Matthew wished he would have just emailed Paul afterwards, explaining that. But he hadn't wanted to deal with Paul anymore. Their interactions were never pleasant. He'd felt it was best for both to just stay in their lanes.

If he had known Paul would commit suicide a little over a year later, of course he would have handled things differently. There was no way to shake the guilt.

However, Paul and Kim were troubled, and they might have done the same thing regardless of the state of Paul and Matthew's relationship. As Kenny said, some people just didn't want to be in this world anymore. He had to stop going back and forth with these 'what ifs.'

And that brought Matthew back to the newborn. Would she have to take on Paul and Kim's debt? That couldn't be right. But then, who would?

Stan didn't have many answers. He was respectful of his loss, but Matthew could tell he was impatient to get this over with.

For the baby's sake, he needed to consult a lawyer. If she was going to be saddled with any kind of debt, he'd want to do all he could to get her out of it.

As for Paul and Kim's possessions, he supposed he could investigate whether selling their things could help pay any debts.

The only thing Matthew had any interest in was a framed photo of Paul and Kim that sat on a bureau in their bedroom. They were semi-smiling, their best attempt at looking happy. A weathered football sat on a paint-chipped rocking chair near the bed. Another reminder that sports was the only connection he and Paul ever had.

After seeing the whole apartment, it finally struck Matthew that nothing indicated a baby would be living there. Did that mean they didn't make a rash last-minute decision? Probably, but he knew it'd be pointless to try and get into their minds. He wished now even more that Paul had reached out to him. He wondered if he didn't on purpose, knowing that having to deal with this would be unpleasant for Matthew. He hated thinking like that. Paul had never been a petty person. Without answers, though, he just didn't know what to think.

Matthew took the photo of Paul and Kim. He would make duplicates so that Allie could have the picture, too. Would she want anything else? Nothing obvious stood out in the apartment. And there was nothing there that indicated who Kim was as a person.

Stan didn't know either. He said he couldn't even remember ever talking to her.

"This is all I'll take," Matthew said as he held the photo of Paul and Kim. "If you have a kid, you can give 'em the football."

Stan nodded. "Thanks."

In his car on the way to the hospital to finally see the baby, Matthew notified the authorities that he wanted Paul and Kim to be cremated. He figured maybe the child would want the urns one day. There was no way of knowing, but if it meant something to her, he'd hate that he didn't at least do that.

Pulling his rental car into the hospital parking lot and getting out, Matthew still had no earthly idea what decision he'd make about the child. He exhaled. A human being's life and future were in his hands. How could anyone, even a decisive person, make this decision?

He made his way slowly into the hospital, hoping dawdling would help clear his mind. It didn't. A nurse directed him to the NICU, which she told him stood for the Neonatal Intensive Care Unit.

Once there, the social worker in charge of Allie's case met him with a gentle smile and a handshake. "Thank you for coming, Matthew. My name is Linda," she said.

He almost instinctively said, "You're welcome," but it didn't feel right so he just gave a small nod.

Linda brought him into an office. A nurse was waiting there, seated behind a desk. She gave him a similar gentle smile, as if a meeting like this wasn't unusual for her. On her blue scrubs was a name tag that said Rebecca.

A quick glance around the room of the serene ocean and landscape paintings made Matthew think this was where all the difficult conversations were had.

Linda and nurse Rebecca went to one side of a desk and sat, with Matthew taking the opposite seat. A vase of plastic flowers obstructed Matthew's view of the nurse so she moved it to the side of the desk by a computer and keyboard.

"Would you like a bottle of water?" Linda asked.

Matthew nodded. His mouth was dry, and it was nice to have a question he could answer.

Rebecca gave a kind smile and went to a mini-fridge, retrieving a small bottle of water. She twisted off the cap and handed it to him, then laughed at herself. "Sorry, I always twist off the tops for patients. Old habits."

Matthew smiled and took a sip of the water, easing his dry mouth somewhat.

"Have you been told anything about the baby?" Linda asked.

"Just that they named her Allie, and she's a preemie," he answered. "How is she doing?"

"She was born with something called broncho-pulmonary dysplasia," the nurse said. "Not entirely uncommon with preemies."

It sounded awful—the poor kid.

"What is it? Will she be okay?" he asked.

"It's a lung condition. Thankfully, it's not a severe case," she said. "Most who have it like she does outgrow it."

"Will she need surgery?"

"No, she'll just need medicines and extra feed-ings to help the lungs heal," the nurse replied. "And because it's not too severe, much of that care can be done on an outpatient basis. She will need to stay here a few weeks, though."

Matthew nodded. He didn't know what to say. It was all just so overwhelming.

"Do you have any idea how you're going to handle things?" Linda asked.

Matthew still didn't. All he could muster was, "My head's just spinning." He took another sip of water.

Linda smiled and nodded. "I'm sure it's a big shock." She and the nurse glanced at each other. He took that to mean they'd need some kind of decision from him. Soon.

"Are you ready to see her?" the nurse asked.

He gave a slight nod, but the mere mention of seeing the baby made his stomach tighten. Seeing her would make it so real. And he felt so uneasy.

Nurse Rebecca got up, and he followed her down a hallway. He hated hospitals. The buzzing light sounds, the mild smell of disinfectant, the look on most people's faces of wanting to be anywhere else.

She brought him into an examination room. It reminded him of the room his own doctor used, except the posters on the wall all dealt with newborn medical issues.

"Have a seat and I'll bring her to you."

He sat. His foot started jiggling nervously, and it was hard to breathe. How did he get here? For the first time he felt a flash of anger at Paul and Kim. How could they do what they did? He knew there were no easy answers, but there had to have been a better path.

But none of that mattered now. He was moments away from meeting a newborn. How did he get here?

Nurse Rebecca finally came back in, holding a small bundle wrapped in a blanket. He couldn't even see the baby yet but could tell she was really small.

"Ready?" she asked, an encouraging smile on her face.

He nodded, his heart beating fast.

She gently placed the blanket with baby Allie in his arms.

He almost gasped. She was so tiny. She looked so vulnerable. He could barely believe he was holding an actual baby.

Mere minutes ago, she only existed in theory. And he couldn't muster any real feelings of attachment. But now, in his arms, she was real. He kept repeating in his head, *You're real*, as he looked at her. So tiny. So vulnerable.

As she looked back up at him, she seemed to form a smile. And his heart melted. He knew he was experiencing something momentous. Something he didn't even know existed. A version of love at first sight. The person he'd loved the most in his life was his mother. He'd never felt that feeling that strongly about someone else before. Until now.

Tears began welling up in his eyes.

"Hi," he said, smiling, as the tears now streaked down his face.

He couldn't stop looking at her. And he also knew, with no equivocation whatsoever, what he wanted to do. Needed to do.

Be her father.

There was not even a remote ounce of indecisiveness. He wanted to give her the very best life he could. And he knew he'd give that effort his all.

He sensed the nurse's eyes on him and looked back up at her. She smiled. She knew his answer. He nodded yes to the unasked question anyway as she handed him a tissue. He wiped his tears and looked back at Allie. He was going to be her daddy. Forever. It was the greatest and most meaningful moment of his life.

# CHAPTER 4

"You're adopting her?" Kenny said, not even attempting to hide his astonishment.

Matthew sat on his bed in his Comfort Suites hotel room, video chatting with Kenny and Sherry.

"Yes," Matthew replied, smiling wide.

"I'm literally speechless," Sherry said. "But you look so happy."

Matthew beamed.

"Brother, if you're happy, I'm happy," Kenny said, "But this is a major decision. Can you handle suddenly being a dad?"

"I know it's major. But yeah, I'm going to handle it."

"What made you … decide this?" Sherry asked.

"Remember how we've talked about having 'without a doubt' moments in your life? And I never seemed to have them?"

"And you had one this time," Sherry said.

Matthew nodded.

"Glad no one bet me on this, 'cause I would've lost," Kenny said. "But congrats." He turned to Sherry. "Our young Matthew is growing up. Who'd a thunk it?"

"And I guess we can't call him 'Mr. Indecisive' anymore," Sherry said, laughing.

"When are you coming home?" Kenny asked.

"Allie has to be in the hospital a little longer. She was a preemie and has a lung condition—but before you freak out—it's treatable."

Neither Kenny nor Sherry said anything. They looked subdued.

"Guys, it's okay. They'll walk me through all the health steps she'll need from me."

They still didn't speak for a moment. Finally, Sherry said, "We'll be here for you. You know that."

"I know. And I'm gonna need it," Matthew said with a chuckle.

On his laptop, he saw that it was a little past 10:30 p.m. "I'm going to get some shut-eye, guys. I have a lot of things I need to take care of tomorrow."

They said their goodbyes and Matthew signed off.

This little room would be his home for the next few weeks. It had no personality, the walls were thin, and being on the first floor of two, he heard feet any time people walked above. The pool outside had a bevy of floating leaves, and no one ever seemed to swim in it. But he thought he'd start sitting out there to get some fresh air at least.

He'd always remember this nondescript hotel and leaf-laden pool and everything about New Mexico because it's where he became a dad.

He looked over at his suitcase on the other bed. It was still unpacked. He decided to keep it that way—but since he didn't bring enough clothes, he'd have to go to the laundromat before returning to Arizona.

He also needed to call Monica to tell her the news. But he was too tired, so it'd have to wait until morning. As he closed his eyes to sleep, he wondered how Monica would react. He'd find out tomorrow.

\* \* \*

"Thanks," Matthew said to Larry over the phone. "I appreciate you understanding." He had filled him in on his situation, and they both agreed it'd be tough for Matthew to continue with his job. He'd have to travel to all the away games during football season. Even if he could afford a full-time nanny, which he didn't think he could, he didn't want to be away from Allie so often. Especially with her health issues.

This was a job he loved, with a salary and health insurance. It dominated his life, and he'd made so many friends there over the years. And yet, he still had no equivocation. He wanted to be Allie's dad; she would come first now. He was actually surprised at how unbothered he was about it.

He was pretty sure he'd have to go back to free-lancing. He thought he had enough savings for at least six months. When he got home, he'd attack the job situation.

He started eating the blueberry muffin the hotel had put out for their complimentary breakfast. He hadn't eaten much on the trip, the nerves sapping his hunger, but he ate a muffin each morning. He always felt he had to eat the free hotel offerings because they jacked up prices in other areas. It was a way, silly, he knew, to cut into those extra expenses.

As he finished the muffin, he sat back and sighed. It was time to call Monica. She deserved an answer. He paced, gathering his thoughts. What if it was an awkward conversation? It wasn't that long ago that he was actually considering leaving Arizona to go to Spain with her, and then Peru, and who knew where else after that? In his heart of hearts, he wished she would want to settle down with him in Arizona and co-parent Allie. But he knew that wasn't what she wanted out of life. They'd have to go their separate ways again.

Matthew dialed her number. She picked up right away.

"Hey. New Mexico treating you okay?" she asked.

"Yeah, pretty well," he answered.

"How's it all going?"

He chuckled a little. "It's going... I have some news, though."

"Okay."

"You may want to be sitting down for this ... I'm adopting Allie."

Monica didn't speak right away before finally saying, "Whoa."

"Whoa, indeed."

"Well, congratulations."

"Thank you."

"You're going to be a dad."

"Yeah. It's crazy sounding."

More silence.

"I think you'll be a good one. You're kind."

"Thanks. I'll do my best."

Another silence.

"I can't really think of what to say," Monica finally said.

"I know."

More silence.

"You mean a lot to me, Monica."

"You mean a lot to me, too."

"Can we stay in touch? I mean, really stay in touch."

"I'd like that."

Matthew breathed a little sigh of relief. "What if we commit to talking or video chatting once a month."

Monica chuckled slightly. "Do you think we can pull that off?"

"I'd like to."

"I'd like to, too. You now have something interesting to talk about besides you taking more pictures of Kenny."

"Wait 'til Kenny finds out I'll be taking pictures of someone more than him."

"Full-on tantrum," she said.

"Fetal position. Hours of screaming. The whole works."

"You should definitely take pictures of that," she said.

He laughed. Then they got quiet again.

"I have to get going," she said. "But keep me updated on everything and … we will talk soon."

"Yes, we will."

They hung up and Matthew leaned back with a sigh. He knew she hid her disappointment as best she could. Once again, he didn't know what their future held. Maybe it wasn't meant to be. Or maybe it wasn't meant to be yet. Only the future could answer that. He did hope they'd keep to their commitment to video chat often.

His thoughts then went to Allie. He wished he went to meet her as soon as he arrived in New Mexico. He was mad at himself that he didn't. For those three days, she had no one in her life who loved her. No one who cared for her. No one who wanted to see that she had the best life ever. He didn't want to ever let her down again. He also couldn't wait to see her again. Everything about being her father excited and frightened him. Every day with her would be a new experience. It was going to be the wildest ride of his life. And that made him smile.

\* \* \*

Weeks passed, and Matthew stayed in New Mexico until Allie was cleared to travel. He visited her every day at the hospital. Getting to hold her was pure joy.

Finally, the hospital pediatrician cleared her to be taken home. A nurse showed him how to feed her formula from a bottle.

"At first, feedings should be every 2–3 hours," the pediatrician said. "But as she gets bigger and her stomach can hold more milk, it'll become every 3–4 hours."

"And I should stick to a cow's milk-based formula?" Matthew asked.

"Correct."

"And the meds for the lung condition—is that all she'll need for that?"

"Yes, keep her on them for the six months. Whatever pediatrician you find in Arizona can evaluate her more closely throughout."

Matthew thanked the doctor and nurses profusely. They had been so patient and professional with him throughout.

As he left the hospital with Allie, he held her at chest level exactly as they showed him, with one hand under her head and another under her bottom. It was as real as it could be now.

On the airplane ride back to Arizona, Matthew sat with a crying Allie as some passengers looked at them. He gave them all the same apologetic look he received from the mom on his flight over.

As he shushed and snuggled her, Allie's perfect pink mouth slowly closed, then opened in a yawn, her eyes shut tight against the bright light of the airplane. Tucking one hand behind her head, he had to chuckle. When he started this trip, he never in a million years thought he'd return as a father.

# CHAPTER 5

"She's so small," Sherry said, a little dismayed as she stood with Matthew and Kenny, looking at Allie sleeping in her crib in a blue onesie.

Their three boys, 4-year-old Jordan and 2-year-old twins Darrell and Darius, looked at Allie, too.

Matthew put the crib in his bedroom, by the side of his bed. The nurses told him that some people preferred having the newborn in another room with a baby monitor, but he wanted her nearby while he slept.

It had been so surreal carrying her into his house. An actual little baby in his home. She was going to grow up here. He'd need to turn his guest room into her bedroom eventually. He had no idea what a little girl's bedroom should look like. Thankfully, there was the Internet—and Sherry. Her crib and bassinet would stay in his room for at least the next six months.

"Looks like a baby to me," Kenny said.

"How long will it take for you to get used to me being a dad?" Matthew asked.

"Maybe by the time she's twenty," Kenny said. "And I'm guessing you won't be hitting the bar for a bit."

Matthew laughed. "Not for a minute."

"Man, is there an app for finding a new drinking buddy?" Kenny said.

"Oh, boo hoo," Sherry said. "You may have to spend more time at home."

Kenny turned to Matthew. "What have you done to my life?"

Matthew laughed again. "Sorry, buddy. I'll get you a Walmart gift card to make up for it."

"You're all heart," Kenny said, chuckling. Then he leaned over Allie's crib. "When you need real life advice, not what you'll get from these two, you come find me. I'll set you straight."

Kenny gave Matthew a hug. "I'm heading out, my man. Sherry can teach you how to nurse her."

"Uh, hello, take the boys," Sherry said. "I'm gonna be here a minute."

"All three?" Kenny said.

"What are they gonna do while I'm showing him stuff?"

Kenny sighed. "Let's go fellas. It's nap time for all of us."

As Kenny left with his sons, he said into his phone, "Siri, how do I find a new best friend?"

Matthew and Sherry chuckled.

"Knucklehead," Sherry said.

"Thanks for not telling him I'm leaving the Cardinals."

"You'll need to tell him soon. He'll talk to Larry at some point."

"He was looking forward to tagging along with me for road games."

"He definitely was."

"All my changes may take him a minute to adjust, especially with him still dealing with retirement."

"Maybe. But you can't worry about it," she said. "You have this little nugget who's gonna occupy all your time."

"Yeah," Matthew said.

They saw Allie wake up. Sherry leaned in towards her. "Hello there, little one." She turned her head back to Matthew. "Can I hold her?"

"Go for it."

Sherry picked Allie up gently, swaying slightly as she held her. "You're a little cutie, aren't you?"

Matthew loved seeing it. Sherry loved her boys and never bemoaned not having a daughter, but he could tell a part of her liked the idea of a girl in their lives.

"Let me see you hold her," Sherry said as she gently handed Allie to Matthew.

As he held her, she said, "Keep her arms closer to her body but allow her legs to move a bit."

He adjusted as she instructed, and it did feel more natural holding her that way. After putting her back in her crib, she started to cry. Matthew exhaled. "She does that a lot."

"All right, time for a Sherry tip. Go get a heating pad."

Matthew went to the hallway closet, pulled the heating pad off the middle shelf, and went back into the bedroom.

"Now turn it on to a light setting and put it in the bassinet."

Matthew did what she said.

"I did this with my boys when they cried. Something about the warmth helps."

Matthew picked up Allie and put her in the bassinet. Her crying slowed and then finally stopped.

"You're a magician," Matthew said.

"It won't always work. Get used to not sleeping a lot."

Matthew chuckled as she gave him a look as if saying, "It won't always be funny."

Before telling Sherry the news, he knew she'd be there for him, in big ways and little.

\*   \*   \*

The first time he had to give Allie her meds was nerve-wracking. He knew how to do it, but not having a nurse nearby made him uneasy.

Sherry wanted to be with him for it, partly out of curiosity but also to be a comforting presence. They stood in his kitchen, with Allie in her bassinet on the table.

"What's the meds called?" Sherry asked.

"Furosemide," he answered as he carefully prepped the oral syringe with the medicine.

"Why do these things have such scary names? They could have called it 'Healing-semide'."

"I couldn't tell ya'," he said. Holding the syringe, he looked at Allie and exhaled. "I got to practice some at the hospital, but something about doing it in front of a nurse made it less nerve-wracking."

He leaned over Allie as he tilted her head at a forty-five-degree angle. With a nervous breath, he stuck the syringe in her mouth. She started naturally sucking on it.

"Look at her. Taking it like a champ," Sherry said.

Matthew took the syringe out and checked to see if it was empty. He looked down at Allie. "Good girl," he said proudly.

Matthew threw the syringe away. "The doctor believes this is the only meds she'll need, but blood tests will have to be done regularly to check that her salt and potassium levels aren't too low."

"Okay, looks like you've got this parenting thing handled so I'll check in with you again in five years," Sherry said.

"I heard 'five minutes.' And I'd like to make that legally binding."

Sherry chuckled. "This is gonna be a ride, that's for sure. But I do have to get back to my little guys— and my big guy who'll complain the loudest if I'm not around enough."

Matthew gave her an appreciative hug. "Just knowing I can come to you is a lifesaver."

"Anytime. And when you're on edge, just remember that same feeling you had when you first saw her. Never let go of that and you'll be fine."

Matthew nodded, appreciating that, as he'd never forget seeing Allie for the first time.

"And my bill will be in the mail," Sherry added, then went to Allie and said, "You take care of your dad for me."

She left, and Matthew sat by Allie's bassinet. "Do you like your new home?" He put his finger in her little hand, and she squeezed. "It's decorated for a 35-year-old man, but I think it suits you, too."

Allie gurgled. "Was that a no on the decorations? Okay, I'll work on something you might like."

*　　*　　*

That night, he put her to bed for the first time with no one else around, gently lowering her into her crib.

He moved to the doorway and turned around to look at her.

He waited for several moments, a little nervously, wanting to make sure she was breathing. It took a bit, but he finally saw it—the gentle rise and fall of her chest.

With that, he relaxed and walked off. It was only 8:00 pm, too early for him to go to sleep. The all-clear regarding her lungs couldn't come soon enough.

He tried watching TV, but all he could think about was Allie in his room, alone. It didn't feel right so he went back to his room and quietly laid down on his bed. He started reading one of the many 'How to' baby books he bought. This one, "Newborns A to Z," gave practical advice, and he wanted to learn it all— but he was having a hard time focusing. Informational words on a page couldn't capture how real it felt to have a little human in a crib mere feet from you.

He'd alternate reading a few pages and looking at her for a few minutes until his eyes started to feel heavy. He put the book down and closed his eyes, but was too wired to sleep.

He repeated this routine the next few nights, and when he did sleep, he'd sometimes wake in a panic, worried she had stopped breathing. But one glance in the crib to see she was fine, and his heart rate would slow. He knew he'd also be a useless mess with no sleep.

"She's gonna be all right," he'd say, measuring his breath and closing his eyes. "She's gonna be all right."

# CHAPTER 6

Having changed Allie's diapers for a few weeks now, Matthew had confidence that he could handle this at least—that was until urine squirted up at him, and he just dodged it before it hit his face.

He was stunned. Was this normal for a girl? Was it something to worry about? He didn't know. Maybe Sherry would.

He quickly wrapped a towel around Allie and called Sherry.

"You're catching me at a crazy time, Matty," Sherry answered. "I'm setting up my new office and have a plumber and electrician here... Everything all right?"

"She peed straight up at me. Is that something girls do?"

Sherry laughed. "Yes, it happens sometimes with girls, too. That's why you called?"

"It freaked me out."

"I'm hanging up," Sherry said. "I hope she pees on you more." Laughing, she hung up.

He looked back down at Allie, feeling relieved but now somewhat wary of being peed on again. He needed a plan. Glancing around his room, he spotted the Patrick Mahomes helmet. It made him laugh as he went over to it, put it on, and tapped the plastic face shield to see if it was sturdy. Satisfied, he went back to Allie and began to re-diaper her.

And on cue, more pee shot up at him, but the plastic face shield blocked it.

"Thought you could outsmart me, huh?"

After affixing the final diaper tab and putting her jammies back on, he texted Patrick, chuckling: *Hey man, thanks again for the helmet. It's coming in really handy.*

Within seconds he received a *???* text back.

Laughing, he texted again: *It's a good pee guard. Got a surprise while changing my baby's diaper.* Patrick sent back laughing emojis.

\* \* \*

"You're breaking my heart, man," Kenny said to Matthew as they stood in front of his new car, a silver Toyota Corolla Cross, which was a little smaller than a regular SUV. "How could you not talk to me before leaving the Cardinals?"

"There's no way I could do the travel. You know that."

"No, I don't. We could have found a way to make it work."

"How? She can't travel with me and I'm not leaving her."

"I would have helped. We could've gotten you a nanny."

"One, I'd never take that big a help. Two, I don't want to leave her for work. At least until her health is okay. But even then, I don't know if I want to."

Kenny sighed. "Breaking my heart. Now neither of us are on the team."

"They'll always consider you on the team."

Kenny harumphed, then looked inside the Corolla's window. "And this. You had a convertible."

"It hurt me too but needed to be done."

"Where will this transition to boring end?"

"I've set up bridge and mahjong games. I told everyone you'd be part of the foursome."

Kenny pretended to dial his cell phone and then spoke into it, "Yeah, police, I think my friend's been body snatched."

"It's a good car," Matthew said, laughing. "Only 28,000 miles on it. Reliable. Practical. Comfortable. And it's a hybrid so I'll save on gas."

They got in the car and Matthew drove off. "See, it's a smooth ride."

"I wish I brought a disguise. Can't have anyone seeing me in this. It'll ruin my rep."

Matthew laughed. "You're killing me, man. You're killing me."

He knew humor was Kenny's way of deflecting his feelings. Matthew's changes were tough on him. Retirement was such a big change, but he at least thought he'd tag along with Matthew a lot during Cardinals' games, so he'd have some semblance of that buddy-sports connection. Now, he wouldn't even have that.

Matthew thought plenty about their friendship. Would it sustain, with his life now being so different? They were more than friends; they were brothers, so he knew it'd never go away. However, compatibility was a huge part of their friendship. With that no longer being there in the same way, he just had no idea what their future would be like.

Matthew drove around the block a few times. He never actually had done that before, but jokes aside, Kenny wanted to experience the ride. He was glad he wouldn't have to move as Gilbert was a very family-ly-friendly neighborhood, and since he owned the house already, his mortgage was manageable. He got a kick out of the copy and paste nature of the homes, as most were like his, a Southwestern style with a well-manicured lawn.

The Corolla would never compare to the smooth ride and look of his Audi, but Matthew did like the feel—and being seated higher was a plus. And the look wasn't bad. It had a certain sleekness to it.

But it was tough handing over the keys to his Audi. He loved that car, and Kenny knew that which is why it hurt him so much, too. Even though he only drove Monica in it once, it reminded him of her as it wasn't that long ago, right before learning about his brother, that they drove that night with the crisp air blowing his hair. Would he ever experience that feeling again?

As Matthew finished the second drive around the block, he said, "No one's fainted seeing you in this yet."

"You should have sold the convertible to me so I could drive by your house every day and make you jealous."

"I have blinds, you know."

"Was the money trade-off at least good?"

"It was pretty good, so it'll help. I'll be selling my memorabilia, too."

"Oh, come on, man."

"Has to be done. I don't want to dip too deep into my savings."

"You'll let me know if you need help, right? Don't do that pride BS thing with me. I'm not talking something big like a nanny."

"I should be good once I start finding gigs. But thanks. The only thing I'm slightly worried about is health insurance. I've priced some things so I can handle it—but I need the gigs."

"Can't Larry give you some gigs?"

"No, he can't do me favors. They have a budget."

"So, what then?"

"I'm looking into something in the nature world. I've always loved nature."

Kenny rubbed his temples, then fake dialed his cell again, "Ya'll police need to find my friend. He's definitely been body snatched."

Matthew chuckled again and drove back to his house, parking on the driveway. He looked at his house. Over the next few days, he'd be selling so many things he really liked. His finances were going to be a major worry until they hopefully no longer were. But he knew he'd be relentless in making sure Allie had everything she'd need.

He and Kenny went into the house to hear Allie start crying. Sherry came into the foyer carrying her.

"When you have a newborn, you have to always enter quietly." She turned to Kenny. "You should know that."

"You could enter like a mime and babies still cry," Kenny said.

Sherry handed Allie to Matthew. "How was the ride?"

"Most boring one ever," Kenny said. "If I ever have insomnia, I'll think of it. Should put me right out."

Allie's crying slowed, then stopped. "Looks like your jokes put her to sleep," Matthew said, smiling.

"You're welcome," Kenny said.

"Shush it up or you'll wake her again," Sherry said. She and Kenny quietly said their goodbyes and

Matthew went into the living room and sat on the couch, cradling Allie. He took a look at all his memorabilia, knowing it'd all be gone soon.

\* \* \*

Matthew sat with Allie on his lap in the living room, on hold with Phil Longham, the editor of the magazine, *Nature Today*.

He looked at the bare walls where all the memorabilia had been. "We're going to put new things up," he said to Allie. "It'll be our things. You'll probably have better taste than me, so can you hurry up and start having opinions."

She hiccupped.

"I'll take that as a yes."

He'd spent years collecting all the signed jerseys, helmets and footballs that he'd just sold. They were all a source of pride and joy, but they couldn't compare to the miracle on his lap. He could always get new memorabilia one day. But he wasn't sure if he would. It'd partly be up to her. He liked the idea of filling up their home with their possessions. She should choose just as much as him.

As he continued to wait on Phil, he thought back to when they met randomly at a sports bar. Phil was a fan of the Cardinals and a fan of his work. At that first meeting, he jokingly said, "We could use someone with your talents at *Nature Today*." Matthew laughed it off, figuring he'd be the Cardinals photographer until he retired. But now he was checking if Phil was joking or not.

"Matthew," Phil said enthusiastically. "Thanks for holding. What do I owe the honor?"

"I'm now a free agent."

"What? You're not with the Cards anymore?"

"I just became a father. A newborn. You can probably hear her gurgling on my knee. So, I can't do the travel anymore."

"Ah, got it. That's amazing about being a father, though, man. So, you're looking for work?"

"I am. And I can only do local stuff for now."

"Well, you know I love your work. We don't have a huge budget, but I may be able to give you some periodic assignments and see where that takes us."

"That would be awesome."

"Actually, I may have something now. Do you like hummingbirds?"

Matthew chuckled. "I do. I like all birds. Even crows."

"Great. Wow, the timing. We were just talking about a hummingbird piece in our next issue, but other photogs we've used were booked. Let me formalize my thoughts about it and we'll talk more." Allie started crying. "Oh no, I think she heard you say you like crows."

"Could be," Matthew said, laughing. "Although, I think someone may need a diaper change."

"I hope you're not the someone."

"Ha! I'm not naming any names."

"We'll talk soon, buddy. Take care."

Matthew started changing Allie while thinking about hummingbirds and the good timing. Maybe that was a sign. "Looks like we're a nature family now."

Even though freelancing wouldn't be ideal, every gig would be something new that he'd probably never photographed before. And nature had no off-season. That part excited him.

But it'd still be tough. And his unwillingness to travel would make it tougher. Having editors who were fans of his work would help so the plan was to make a list of all he'd met and then doggedly communicate with each until, hopefully a full-time position would materialize again.

The worry was, though, would he get enough gigs to pay the bills in the meantime? Allie's well-being depended on him entirely. That made it scary. Like walking a tightrope without a safety net.

# CHAPTER 7

"I wish I saw her pee on you," Monica said, laughing. "That would've made my day."

Matthew adjusted his laptop, making sure that Allie was visible on the screen. This was Monica's first time meeting her.

"I bet it would have," he replied. "If you visit, maybe you'll see it in person."

"Tempting," she said, laughing again. "But for now, our video chats will have to do."

"Yeah," he replied. "When she's older, maybe we'll find you out there wherever you'll be."

Monica got silent. Then, "Yeah, maybe."

"Would you be okay with us visiting one day?"

"Yeah, of course." She got silent again. "I wasn't sure if I'd mention this, but I may have found someone."

Matthew took a moment. "That's … terrific. Of course I want you to share it. I meant it about being friends."

"I know, but still."

He nodded. "Tell me about him."

"His name's Juan. From Spain so I'm on his turf. He does freelance gigs like me."

"Is he going to Peru with you?"

"That's what we're figuring out."

"I guess I'll know by our next chat."

"Probably. I'm glad you still want to chat."

"Of course."

"And thank you for letting me see your little bundle there."

"Absolutely. I want you to see her grow up. From afar, of course."

They said goodbye and Matthew logged off, leaning back. Her news took him by surprise, and he didn't love hearing it. He knew that was selfish and that he had no right to feel that way, but he did.

He looked down at Allie and smiled. She gave a little smile back. "I know you don't understand me yet, but I have no regrets. None, none, none." He kissed her forehead, and she gave another little smile.

\*   \*   \*

Life with Allie in the newborn stage felt like he was living in a loop. Lot of changing diapers and feedings—both every three hours, giving her meds at the same time every day, stealing naps whenever he could. The days melded together.

One joy was their mini photo sessions. He'd photograph her in as many fun baby costumes as he could find. His favorite was one where she looked like she was in the middle of the sun. Each costume was adorable and made him chuckle, and they made for some fantastic pictures. These would be memories he'd treasure.

The exhaustion, however, was real. Everyone said it would be, so it wasn't a surprise. But knowing it was coming and experiencing it were two different things. It was 3:15 am and Matthew sat and held Allie in her little pink blanket. She had finally stopped crying but now let out a soft whimper. He gave a soothing shush sound as he gently bounced her rhythmically. The coffee mug next to him was empty, but his body was too tired to get up for a refill.

As Allie quieted, his head drooped, begging for sleep. But he couldn't yet. He needed to make sure she was asleep for at least a few minutes before he'd put her back in the crib. And then hope this sleep lasted, at least a few hours.

She cried a lot and the frequency worried him. During her last visit to her pediatrician, Dr. Bauer said her crying was more than usual, but they ran all the tests, and she didn't appear to be allergic to her food, or meds, or anything else.

Still, Matthew couldn't stop worrying that she was in distress in some way. He asked the doctor if the crying was related to her lung condition. He didn't think so, but he couldn't say for sure. And he said until her six-month checkup, which was now just a month away, he wouldn't know if the meds had healed her lungs like they hoped.

Matthew also made the mistake of looking things up on the Internet. While occasionally helpful, it often sent him down loopholes that scared him even more.

He didn't know if there was a worse feeling than not knowing if your child was okay or not.

*   *   *

Matthew's phone alarm went off. It was time for Allie's meds. He was becoming more comfortable using the syringe to deliver them. And she handled it like a champ, sucking every last drip out of it.

This time when she was done, he made a funny face, and she let out a little laugh which overjoyed him. He stared at her, so in love with this little girl. Who would she become? What would her voice sound like? What would be her favorite food? What if she liked something like chickpeas, which he hated? He was fascinated. What would their relationship be like? Would she like him? What would her personality be? Her parents' mental health issues lingered in the back of his mind. Was that something a person inherited?

He planned on giving her the happiest environment he could, but if depression was an inherited condition, what could he do about that?

What he didn't like about his thoughts were they often devolved into worrying. Not just about her mental health but her physical health, too. He felt so helpless about her lung condition. She showed no signs that it was an issue, but there were no guarantees.

The way he put her to bed on her first night had become his routine. Standing in the doorway, waiting to see her breathe before moving on.

When the worrying happened, he fought to think positively. What kinds of things would make her laugh? What music would she like? Would she like sports, like him? Would she like dresses and dolls? He didn't know, but he couldn't wait to find out.

# CHAPTER 8

The six-month mark arrived. Matthew sat with Allie in one of Dr. Bauer's examination rooms, waiting for him to say whether she should stay on the meds, which, if so, meant her lung condition hadn't normalized.

She had been crying so much lately that he dreaded what he may hear. Nervous wasn't a strong enough word for how he felt.

He smiled slightly at how most of the room was made to be kid friendly. The rubberized part of the stethoscope was light blue and had small smiley stickers on it. There was a flat scale with a cushion so a baby could lie comfortably on it, and on the wall, there was an eye chart which had cute animal pictures instead of letters.

With Allie on his lap, Matthew put his finger in her hand, and she squeezed, something they often did to connect. This time it felt more meaningful.

Dr. Bauer walked in and sat. "Her lungs look good."

Matthew smiled brightly and sighed. Tears welled up in his eyes, but he held them back. Later, they would pour out.

"Her immune system may still be a little low for a while, so I want you to give her 400 IU of Vitamin D every day."

"Will her immune system always be low?"

"It usually normalizes at some point, but each child is different for when. The Vitamin D should help."

"She's still crying so much."

"We've run all the tests, and she appears healthy. Some babies just cry more."

"Is it a personality thing? That she's more sensitive to things?"

"That's very possible. Once she gets older, you'll be able to determine that more."

As relieved as he was at the doctor's diagnosis, he couldn't help thinking, *What if the doctor's wrong?* With the insurance he was able to procure he wouldn't be able to afford a second opinion. He'd never forgive himself if her lungs weren't actually healthy.

Sherry saw his worry and made an appointment for her with a different specialist. He was overwhelmed with gratitude. And when the specialist confirmed her lungs were good, he could finally relax. He thanked Sherry and Kenny profusely, but they each jokingly told him to shut up, as, of course they'd do this for him and Allie.

After the specialist's confirmation, when Matthew arrived home, he grabbed Allie's syringe and carried it and her over to the trash can. With pleasure, while holding her in one arm, he threw the syringe in the trash. Then he made her little hand wave bye to it.

\* \* \*

Each new day brought a new experience, whether certain clothes didn't fit her anymore, or she made an entirely different laughing sound, or she slept one night without crying and then the next wouldn't stop crying.

As for money, he wasn't overly concerned as he started picking up more gigs for nature shots, mostly from Phil, who really liked his hummingbird photos. To capture them, he had taken Allie on their first road trip, a three-hour drive south to Ramsey Canyon Preserve near the southern border between Arizona and Mexico. It was known as the 'Hummingbird Capital of the World.'

Allie did well on the drive, and he was curious to see how she reacted to being outside while he photographed the birds. She ended up only crying once, for a short bit. Maybe the great outdoors was good for her, or perhaps it kept her interest. Or maybe she was just having a good day, which also happened occasionally. He had no way of knowing. He couldn't wait for the day she could speak and tell him anything that was bothering her.

And even though she couldn't understand him, he talked her through his process as if she did understand—because maybe she did. So, he explained how he used a 200 mm telephoto lens on a tripod to get good close-ups of the birds without being too close to disturb them. And using a shutter speed of 1/1000 to freeze, he was able to capture their rapid wing beats as they hovered near flowers.

It was fascinating observing them and trying to anticipate their movements. It differed from capturing athletes doing great athletic things, and since that had been what he experienced the last ten years, taking these pictures was like getting to flex a muscle he hadn't flexed in a while.

As he drove home, Allie cried more in the back seat. It'd been a long day for her, and maybe she started having motion sickness. Again, the not knowing drove him crazy.

But he knew he'd want to take her on shoots when she was old enough to know what was going on and hoped she enjoyed the experience as much as he did. But he wouldn't force it. If it wasn't her thing, they'd do other activities together.

He never knew if the freelancing opportunities would dry up, though. Phil hoped to add him full-time as *Nature Today* was growing on and offline, but he said it might be a year or so before that happened. So, he'd stay frugal for now.

Allie still stayed in a crib in his bedroom, but he had begun changing his guest room to her bedroom.

He thought she should pick the color scheme when she could, but for now he went with a light purple for the walls.

When she was fourteen months old, she uttered her first words. "Dada." Well, not officially. Her first words were actually gibberish—but he liked to believe she was trying to say "Dada." But when she finally did say it clearly, he smiled ear to ear. He knew it was unbelievably cliché, but it was also by far the most likely because he'd constantly tell her he was "Dada."

Kenny happened to be over when it happened, and he shook his head as Matthew ran around the room celebrating as if he had scored a touchdown.

"Man, it's cheating if that's the only word you ever try to get her to say."

"You're just mad 'cause all yours said 'Mama' first."

"That's 'cause Sherry cheated, too."

"So, cheaters do win sometimes," Matthew said, laughing.

"I fear the nonsense you're gonna be teaching this child."

At sixteen months, she took her first steps, which he captured on video. They were like little weebly-wobbly steps, and she stopped halfway through on her way over to him as if to take in the experience, then she forged on the rest of the way over. He stopped filming and scooped her up for a huge hug. He couldn't believe how happy the moment made him.

That night he cradled her, so grateful. Grateful that she was healthy. Grateful that she was in his life. He couldn't wait for what the rest of their life would be together.

# PART 2

# CHAPTER 9

Matthew sat at his laptop, uploading all the photos he recently took of Arizona's wildflowers at Picacho Peak State Park. He had been on staff at *Nature Today* for a little over two years now, grateful the freelancing days were behind him.

As he typed an email to Phil letting him know most of the flowers were pink Storksbills and royal-blue Tall Mountain Larkspurs, loud thunder boomed. So loud it caused Matthew to jump a little.

And then he heard Allie cry down the hall. He headed towards her room as another loud thunderclap boomed.

He entered her room to see her wide awake, crying and really frightened. And the thunder was loud—louder than he could remember hearing it.

Allie was four now and still small for her age.

"Hey, it's okay," Matthew said, sitting beside her and turning on the bedside light. "Thunder's just loud. It won't hurt us."

A flash of lightning just hit outside the closest window, followed by more loud thunder. Allie cried harder and grabbed Matthew, holding him tight. Her shoulder-length brown hair pressed against the side of his chest as if she could escape from the thunder somehow by burrowing into him.

"I know it's scary. But I promise it won't hurt us." He twirled his finger into her hair, where it curled up a little at the edges. Sometimes that soothed her. "You know what, I have an amazing picture of lightning I once took."

Scrolling through his phone, Matthew brought up a dazzling picture of lightning. "I was outside when I took this."

Allie looked at the picture on the phone, which calmed her a little. Her crying slowed and finally stopped as her curiosity kicked in.

"Were you scared?" she asked.

"A little. But there's a big word called adrenaline."

She tried repeating "adrenaline" but missed most of the middle part of the word.

He smiled at her attempt. "Close enough," he said. "When things are a little scary it can actually be exciting sometimes. So even though I was a little scared, I put that aside and took my pictures. And I got this. One of my favorites."

More lightning, followed by thunder. She held him tight again, but this time she didn't cry.

"And the thunder noise," he said. "That's what the lightning sounds like."

"Why doesn't it come at the same time?" she asked.

"There's something called the speed of light," he answered. "And the speed of sound. And light is faster than sound. Make sense?"

She shook her head no.

"Yeah, to me either," he said. "But scientists say that's what happens and they're really smart. Maybe not as smart as me 'cause I know everything about everything that ever existed."

She giggled. By this point, she knew he was a little silly.

"Nuh-uh," she said.

"What? You don't think I'm the smartest person ever, ever, ever?" he asked, feigning offense.

"I think Ms. Sherry's smarter than you 'cause she's always showing you how to do things."

"She is smarter than me. Okay, I'm the second smartest ever, ever, ever."

She giggled again and he kissed her on the head. She was a sweet and curious little girl with the cutest little laugh, but also one who had anxiety issues. Things scared her easily, and she was quick to cry. And so many things scared her: insects, loud noises, people, darkness, the water at the pool. Dr. Bauer believed it was just who she was, and maybe it would lessen as she got older.

He'd tried a lot of things to help her anxiety, and while humor could sometimes ease a situation, he had wondered if music might help even more. It certainly helped him. He hadn't tried the music route yet as an anxiety remedy, but now was a good time to try. He thought of one of his favorite songs, and best at easing any of his anxiety. Bob Marley's *Three Little Birds (Don't Worry About a Thing)*.

"Y'know, there's a song I listen to when I get worried about things. Maybe it can be our song."

He brought the Bob Marley song up on his phone, put it on her bedside table and picked her up, slow dancing with her as he sang along with the song.

*"Don't worry, about a thing,*
*'Cause every little thing, is gonna be alright.*
*Singing, don't worry, about a thing,*
*'Cause every little thing, is gonna be alright!"*

The lightning and thunder continued but she was more focused on the fun song and dancing as she giggled throughout. He danced them past the stuffed animals that she had placed on a rocking chair in the corner, then by the bookshelf filled with children's books—which also had the two urns of Paul and Kim on the top shelf, then by the bin filled with toys, and finally up to the small table and chair near the door.

He slow spun her a few times—then put her on top of the table and twirled her before picking her back up and slow dancing more before putting her back in bed. They finished singing the song together.

*"Don't worry, about a thing,*
*'Cause every little thing, gonna be all right."*

The lightning and thunder had slowed as the song ended.

He tucked her in and kissed her on the head again.

"You get some sleep for me?" he asked.

She nodded with a smile, then curled up with a white fluffy teddy bear and closed her eyes. Before he shut off the light, he looked around the room and smiled. Her room brought him joy. And she chose most of the things in it, including keeping the light purple color scheme.

He walked out, closing the door about halfway. As he looked back at her, he was grateful for being able to ease her this time, but he couldn't shake the worry that she continued to become so upset in the first place. Would she always be like this? Was there anything he could do, especially to help her cope when he wasn't around?

He'd thought about therapy for her. Reading about it, there were mixed thoughts on how appropriate it was for a four-year-old. But he decided if it could help her at all, it'd be worth a try, even if his insurance wouldn't cover it. So, he started looking for therapists.

# CHAPTER 10

"Man, she ain't a baby anymore," Kenny said, frustrated. "And way past all her health stuff. You can't keep missing the trip."

Matthew sat with Kenny and Sherry in their back-yard patio area, watching Jordan, now 8, and Darrell and Darius, now 6, play football with Allie by handing her the ball and letting her run with it while they blocked. She laughed throughout, really enjoying it.

"I think she'd kill your vibe if I took her," Matthew joked.

Kenny shot him a 'stop joking' look, but it made Matthew chuckle anyway. It was the time of year for the annual week-long fishing trip with Donovan, Marvin, and Charlie—the former being part of the PR team for the Cardinals, and the latter two being former Cardinals' teammates of Kenny's. Matthew used to go with them to Bartlett Lake in the Tonto National Forest, but once he adopted Allie, he stopped.

"It could double as a work thing," Kenny said. "Your nature mag would love our trip. We got a river, trees, all them furry little things that eat nuts. C'mon."

"I'm just not ready," Matthew replied.

"Sherry will look after her," Kenny said.

"I will?" Sherry asked, not appreciating him just deeming this.

"Our fishing trip's a big deal," Kenny argued. "All the boys need to be there. Otherwise, it ain't the same."

"I told ya' I'll do a day trip but not a week," Matthew said.

"That ain't a trip," Kenny said with a dismissive wave.

"Lay off him, K," Sherry said. "You're being selfish."

"I'm not," he said. "You're not grasping what this trip is to us."

"You still go," she replied. "With the other fellas. Catchin' your fish. Probably drinkin' too much. Probably makin' jokes I'd crack you over the head with the frying pan for... Not missing anything."

"Do you miss it?" Kenny asked Matthew.

Matthew gave a small, conflicted smile.

"See," Kenny said to Sherry.

"I miss you guys," Matthew said. "But I don't miss it more than I'd miss being away from her."

"You will at some point, man," Kenny said. "Then you're gonna beg us to go sometime. And we may take a vote on your ass."

Kenny finished his beer and headed inside.

"If you did want to go, I got you," Sherry said to Matthew.

"I know," he replied, and they dapped it up.

Sherry and he continued to watch the kids play. Matthew loved that the boys had become close with Allie. It was the one other place besides his home she felt comfortable. And unlike Matthew's small back-yard, theirs was huge with a large grass area for them to run around freely, a half basketball court, and a small playground with a swing set, slide, and sandbox.

Matthew looked back into the house, realizing Kenny wasn't coming back out. He felt bad that Kenny was upset by him missing the trip, but the mere idea of being apart from Allie for a week made him feel queasy. And he didn't think it was because of her 'being scared of things' issue. It was because he didn't want to be away from her.

"So, how's it going with her therapist?" Sherry asked.

"Allie likes her. So that's good. She mentioned hypnosis and that scared me a little."

"Four seems young for that."

"Yeah, we'll see. The therapist said that there's not always something you can change about a person, but managing things is doable."

"I've known people with anxiety who have been in therapy for fifteen years. And they still have it."

"But are they managing it?"

"Who knows?"

"Yeah. I'm glad I'm trying it for her, though."

"I think she'll be just fine. She's too big a sweetheart."

Matthew smiled at that as the football rolled over to them. He picked it up and started running so the kids could chase him, which they did with great exuberance. He wished he could bottle these joyful moments for Allie and have her take it with her when he was not around.

\*     \*     \*

And Allie could have used that joy bottle the next day at preschool when a boy teased her about one of her drawings and made her cry.

Even before enrolling her in preschool, he wondered if it was the best thing to do since she was so sensitive. Kids in school made other kids cry all the time. But it happened fairly frequently with Allie. He hated that she could get upset so easily, but would it be even more harmful if he sheltered her from it by homeschooling? He thought it best that she experience school and interacting with others—hoping that it acclimated her in some way.

But her school difficulties were happening more frequently. At least a few times each week, her teacher, Ms. Kenneson, told him about another crying episode. It happened enough that she wanted to meet and discuss it—so they met after school in the hallway outside her classroom while Allie sat inside drawing.

"She's one of the more sensitive kids I've worked with," Ms. Kenneson said. "Things seem to scare or upset her easily."

"I know," Matthew replied. "I have her with a therapist. But she's more or less fine at home. I'm wondering if she's just not ready for preschool."

"From a learning development standpoint, she is. In fact, she's ahead of most of the others. And she's a total sweetheart. But she seems to have trouble with how the other kids are, especially ones that are a little rowdy and don't have good attention spans. Their behavior seems to upset her."

"That's my dilemma. If I take her out of school, how will she develop social skills when dealing with others in life if she never actually has to deal with others in life?"

He knew there were other ways of socialization for homeschooled children outside of school, but for someone like Allie, he didn't think occasional socialization was best.

"I get it's a tough choice." Ms. Kenneson paused before continuing. "She has no other siblings, right?"

With how she said it, Matthew sensed she was tiptoeing around another subject, especially since she already knew Allie was an only child. She also knew he was a single father. It stood out as all the other kids in Allie's class were dropped off and picked up at school by their mothers.

Did Ms. Kenneson think that Allie not having a mom might have something to do with her socialization issues? Or that something about her home life was contributing to her sensitivity? Perhaps he was being paranoid, but he suddenly felt a little uncomfortable as he shifted in his seat.

"Yeah, no siblings."

Ms. Kenneson looked down a little nervously and fumbled with some papers in Allie's file. She must have sensed he was uncomfortable with her question.

"Like I said, she's seeing a therapist—and she thinks this may just be Allie's personality, regardless of anything else. My brother and his wife had anxiety issues. Seems like she inherited some of it."

Ms. Kenneson didn't press anything further. She ended the meeting by saying, "I'll keep letting you know how she's doing."

Matthew left the meeting depressed. And he was even less certain about whether he should keep Allie in school.

\* \* \*

"You promised me you wouldn't do this to yourself," Sherry said to Matthew as she was about to hit a golf ball at the Legacy Driving Range.

He stood behind, waiting for his turn. "I just feel helpless."

Allie's last week at school was a bad one. She had had several more crying instances: someone teased her about her hair, someone didn't share something, and a bee almost stung her. It felt like an incident was happening almost every day, and Matthew was down about it.

"That's half of parenting." She settled into her stance then struck the ball, which sliced and landed about a hundred twenty yards away. She shook her head. "Mopey Matty's got me off my game."

She looked at him and saw that he didn't step forward. "Are you competing today?"

"Not in the mood. You keep going."

"Matty. C'mon. This is not good."

"I feel like I'm failing her," he said, his eyes getting watery.

"You're not failing her. We give it all we have. That's all we can do as parents. You're doing that."

"But if she's always scared or nervous or anxious— what kind of life will she have?"

"Stop it. Don't do this to yourself."

He took a deep breath, which helped calm him.

"Let's sit for a few so you can clear your head," she said, leading them to a bench. "I want to whoop your butt fair and square."

He finally allowed himself a small chuckle.

"There you go. Get out of your head."

Sherry and he started competing at things again when Allie began preschool. Back in college, they used to compete at video games, but now it was air hockey, darts, or who could make the most free throws in a row or hit better at the driving range.

"Every parent has these moments," Sherry said. "It comes with it."

"I know. But when things happen, it's still hard."

"You need more balance in your life, bub. Allie and your work occupy too much of your headspace."

"Adding more to my headspace could also make things worse."

"Nah, humans need balance."

He gave her a quick glance, then stifled a smile.

"What, you have a thought on balance?"

"I was just thinking I know a human who could use more balance on her drive," he said. "That last slice was awful."

"Uh, hello, who kicked your butt in air hockey the other day?"

"And what about last week in darts?"

"It's only a matter of time before I take that crown, too," she said.

"You know you can't beat the Bullseye Baby."

"The Bullseye Baby?" she said, chuckling. "That has to be the most embarrassing nickname anyone's ever given themselves."

They both laughed.

"But don't change the subject. Dating would be good for you."

She didn't mention Monica this time, but for at least a year she felt he wasn't over Monica and that's why he wasn't dating. He denied it, but she wasn't wrong. Whenever he thought of meeting someone new, he'd think of Monica and wish he was with her. Especially since she'd been single for the last six months and their video chats had become flirtier.

She had only had the one stab at a relationship several years ago, Juan from Spain, but it fizzled quickly, she said.

Sherry got a text and groaned. "Kenny's asking if he's gotta do the speech I set up for him tomorrow."

Matthew hadn't actually talked to Kenny in a few weeks. They didn't hang out as much and neither seemed to be in the mood for it. Kenny had even stopped watching football, which Matthew understood, but it saddened him. For the majority of Kenny's life, football was his identity. If it hurt him so much even to watch it, then he was struggling mentally. But with Allie's issues keeping him occupied, Matthew didn't have the mental capacity to be there for him, which he felt guilty about.

"He's good at speaking. Why does he want out?"

"He doesn't want to do anything lately."

"His ankle still bothering him?"

"Yeah, may need another surgery."

Sherry got silent. If she didn't want to talk about Kenny, he wouldn't press.

"Maybe we skip today and just get some fries," she said.

"Works for me."

"We'll say you defaulted and give me the win."

He laughed. "You're paying for the fries then."

As they got up to leave, Matthew got a text from Phil: *What do you think of Denmark?*

Intrigued, Matthew called him, but it went to voicemail. Phil then texted again: *Can't talk just yet. May be a gig there.*

Matthew showed Sherry the text exchange.

"Would you actually go there with Allie?"

"I don't know. I'll need to talk to him first."

As they left, he really didn't know. He'd need details before developing too much of a thought about it. But it made him think of Monica. She was in Berlin right now. Would they be able to meet up? Possibly seeing her in person excited him. He couldn't wait to talk to Phil to learn more.

# CHAPTER 11

"Oh my God, I'd love that," Monica said as Matthew video chatted with her. "I have two days free in my schedule during your second week there."

"Awesome. I was hoping it could work with our dates."

Before calling Monica, he finally talked to Phil, who told him he had secured a grant to send a photographer to Denmark for two weeks, and his first choice was Matthew. He didn't say yes yet; he wanted to talk to Monica first.

"It's been a minute since I've been to Denmark," she said. "I love a good Frikadeller."

"Is that food or some kind of street performance?" Matthew asked, laughing.

"I'm going to let you figure that one out," she said, also laughing.

"I better remember to Google it then so I don't embarrass myself."

"I'm more worried about you embarrassing Allie."

"She has to get used to that sooner or later."

Monica laughed again.

"She'll be excited to meet you in person."

"Yeah, me too." Monica took a pause, and he did, too. One of them needed to bring up the elephant in the room.

She finally said, "So … is this a friend's visit?"

He didn't answer right away. He knew expecting them to restart an actual relationship wasn't rational. There were so many barriers to that happening. And yet, if he was being truthful, he wanted that. Finally, he said, "I don't know what kind of visit it is. I just know I want to see you."

"I want to see you, too," she said. Then, with emphasis, "But…"

"Yeah, Allie… She's my priority… Does that make you hesitant?"

"No. I just don't want to confuse things with us. Or confuse her."

"Yeah. This time it'll be different."

"Maybe we just don't label it," she said.

"We'll just enjoy each other. How about that?"

She chuckled lightly. "Yes, let's go with that."

"So, we'll see each other soon."

"Looking forward to it."

They smiled and signed off. Matthew leaned back. He didn't know what those two days together would be like. But they'd be together. And from that, anything was possible.

He still needed to tell Phil he was in. He had been leaning towards going, but if Monica couldn't meet them, he wasn't sure how he'd feel.

And it had taken him a few days of going back and forth about whether the trip would be good for Allie. Being away from her doctor made him nervous. What if her immune system was still low? And she'd miss two weeks of school. Would that be difficult for her in some way? He didn't know. Sherry teasingly exclaimed, "Mr. Indecision is back."

He knew part of his indecision was Monica. Was she the main reason he wanted to go? If so, was it okay that she was the main reason? Even if she was, he knew he'd never go if it was detrimental to Allie in any way, but there was no way to really answer that without going.

He had waited before video chatting with Monica to try and answer the Allie question. She'd see and experience so many new things. She'd have the kind of memories from a trip like this that a young child could actually remember. To deny her that, because of his fears, felt unfair. And he also started believing, without any clear information to do so, that a positive experience like this could possibly even alleviate her anxiety. That made sense to him—for the more she understood the world, maybe the less afraid of it she'd be.

Life was a gamble, and he had to pick something. He ultimately believed that it'd be good for her. At least he hoped.

Either way, they'd be going.

# CHAPTER 12

"Allie, I promise they won't hurt you," Matthew said as Allie held tightly to his leg, crying and shaking.

They were at the Bornholm Butterfly Park, their first excursion in Denmark. Inside the glass-enclosed building—which resembled a large greenhouse—they were surrounded by over a thousand brightly colored butterflies of all shapes and sizes flitting around trees, shrubs, and flowering plants.

He knew insects scared her, but she had never been frightened of butterflies before. In fact, she often commented on how beautiful they were. With so many flitting around, though, she acted as if they may start attacking.

A butterfly with maroon and yellow-trimmed wings flew near them. Matthew put his finger out and the butterfly landed on it. "See, they're friendly."

She still held his leg but lessened her crying.

"Do you trust me?" he asked.

She gave a little nod, yes, whereupon he slowly moved the butterfly down toward her.

"Look how friendly he is," Matthew remarked. "I think this is called a Mourning Cloak Butterfly."

He brought it down to her level so she could see it clearly. It took a few moments, but she stopped crying.

"I think he likes you," Matthew said.

"The wings are pretty," she said as her curiosity kicked in.

"Yeah, they are," he replied. "Want to see him closer?"

He slowly moved the butterfly towards her face. Her eyes widened.

"I promise he won't hurt you. He's our friend."

He continued ever so slowly to bring the butterfly closer to her. She now seemed transfixed, even more so when he carefully placed the butterfly on her nose. Her mouth opened in awe as she stood there with it on her.

Matthew then leaned in, giving a soft little blow to the butterfly, and it flew off. Allie squealed, "Bye-bye!" in delight as she waved goodbye.

Matthew smiled proudly at her. "That's my girl."

He picked her up and walked further into the park. The air, while humid, smelled so sweet from all the foliage, ranging from the Bottlebrush trees with their bright red flowers to the Firebush shrubs with their orange-red tubular flowers to standalone Zinnia and Verbena flowers.

Allie now gazed in wonderment at all the butterflies, each seeming to carry a tiny piece of stained-glass artwork on its wings.

He took out his camera, having brought his Sony A1 on the trip, and positioned it so she could see the shot on the digital screen. Then he motioned for her to press the red-trimmed button. She giddily took the shot as butterflies danced around them and giggled every time a new one landed on her.

They spent about an hour there, getting so many great pictures of butterfly closeups and group shots and those in mid-flight. She loved pressing the button on his camera to take the picture, and he decided before their next stop he'd get her a disposable camera, the kind he once had as a kid. The idea of her very own camera thrilled her.

When they left, he bought Allie a butterfly picture book from the gift shop. She'd flip through the book, finding butterflies that looked like ones they encountered, each time saying, "I found another one."

They were just two days into the trip, but they'd already experienced a lot. It began with the airplane ride where Allie saw snow on Arizona's Mazatzal Mountains and the Atlantic Ocean from high above. Then, driving from Copenhagen Airport to their hotel, they saw farmland and Fjords. The word Fjord made her curious and she asked what it was.

"It's a long, narrow portion of the sea that's between high cliffs. The one we're seeing is called the Roskilde Fjord."

"It looks like a river."

"It's kind of similar. It was once a river valley that was flooded by seawater."

Allie turned to him with a smile. "You *do* know everything about everything."

He laughed. "Well, I kind of cheated by studying a lot of Denmark before we flew here."

Even the ferry ride they took to get to the island of Bornholm was an exciting experience for her, mainly because she thought it was funny that cars got to ride the ferry, too.

Their hotel, which they picked together because they enjoyed saying its name, Comwell Roskilde, was also exciting for her because she'd get to sleep on her own queen-sized bed, an "Adult bed" as she called it, with really big pillows.

Everything was a first for her, and since she was so curious every experience was meaningful. To him as well because not only did he love the experience but seeing it through her eyes made it even more memorable.

*   *   *

Matthew and Allie lay in the grass at their next stop, Matthew King's Garden. She found it funny that it had the same name as him.

Matthew positioned his camera to capture a shot of a Kingfisher. He was thrilled, as this was probably Denmark's most colorful bird—a glistening metal-like turquoise.

He excitedly explained to Allie that this was a real treat because Kingfishers were quite shy and often difficult to spot.

She said, "Like me," which surprised him.

"Why do you think they're like you?"

"My therapist said I was shy and that there was nothing wrong with that."

"She's right, there is nothing wrong with it."

"And I'm difficult to spot 'cause I'm the smallest in my class."

"That makes sense. So, you're like a Kingfisher— one of the best birds ever."

That made her giggle.

As they walked through the perfectly manicured gardens, she kept saying, "It's so pretty and smells so good."

"Should we build this in our backyard?"

"Yes," she said, laughing. "But ours isn't big enough."

"We'll make a tiny one then."

She smiled. "Is Monica coming today?"

"In a few days. Are you excited?"

"Yeah. She'll be real. I can touch her."

"I'm sure she'll give you a big hug."

The closer they got to seeing Monica, though, the more he started developing irrational fears over it. The main one being what if Allie liked her so much that she started questioning why she didn't have a mommy in her life.

He'd had that talk with her before and she never expressed any disappointment, but she also never experienced spending quality time with him and a woman. Would she now think that she had been missing something?

He wanted to slap himself when he had thoughts like that. He couldn't wait to see Monica, so worrying about how Allie might or might not react to the situation would only dampen things. And yet, he couldn't stop himself from thinking about it.

And then he'd think about how the reunion would transpire. Would things turn romantic again once Allie went to sleep? Or would they feel uncomfortable with that and just talk? He played out in his mind how he wanted it to go. That she'd love the dynamic of being with him and Allie so much that she'd want to make that permanent. Was that unlikely? He didn't know, but it didn't feel impossible.

*   *   *

"Get your camera ready," Matthew said to Allie as they sat at the edge of Stevns Klint, a white chalk and limestone cliff. Just then, the most amazing sunrise he'd ever seen emerged over the horizon.

"Wow," Allie said as the sky became a lush canvas of orange and gold, and the warmth of the sun's rays enveloped them.

"Wow, is right," he said as he took pictures with his camera, and she followed suit with her disposable one.

It was cute how she paid attention to the way he would shoot things, like if he shot at a certain angle or got down on one knee to steady a shot, she'd do the same. He remembered how thrilled he was when he followed his mother around, mimicking how she photographed things. Allie showed the same exuberance.

As the sun continued to climb in the sky, it felt as if a golden glow was spreading across the landscape. They sat back at the cliff's edge and watched, soaking it all in.

"Can you believe the sun's actually 93 million miles away from us?"

"It's moving," Allie replied in a wondering way.

"It looks like it's moving," he said. "But we're really the ones who are moving."

"I don't feel it," she said.

"You just have to trust it," he said as they took more pictures. This time, instead of following his lead, she started experimenting by changing the angles of her camera. He chuckled and said, "A chip off the old block."

"What does that mean?"

"It means you and me are alike."

"Of course. You're my daddy." That made him smile.

She hadn't cried since the initial butterfly meeting, but that changed when she scraped her left knee slipping on gravel as they were leaving the cliffs. A good chunk of her knee's skin came off.

This was where Sherry's voice always rang in his head. "Kids fall, kids get hurt, kids cry." He knew that, but he still hated it. He couldn't fix everything, but as he cleaned her wound and bandaged her up, he wanted her to know he'd always try to fix things.

One of his earliest memories was falling off a skateboard on his family's driveway and his father looked disappointed when he cried. "Just go get a damn band-aid," he said to Matthew. "And if you keep crying, do it in your room."

That was another recurring conversation with Sherry. Her parents didn't coddle her either and she wondered if that was the better way to handle things, because when kids eventually had to venture out into the real world on their own, there'd be no coddlers.

They didn't have an answer because it also felt completely heartless not to care when your child was hurt. They both agreed it was best to aim for a middle ground. He, of course, had more trouble with that than Sherry. Definitely more trouble with it than Kenny, although he'd tell Kenny he'd feel differently if he had a daughter. Kenny waved it off, but Matthew believed he was right.

Not coddling was difficult for him. He had always felt others' emotions and fed off it. If they were happy, he could be happy. If they were sad, he felt down. And with Allie, that emotion feeding intensified by a thousand.

Ultimately, he decided that being someone who leaned more towards coddling was who he was and would probably always be. And he hoped it wouldn't hinder her when it was her time to face the real world on her own.

After putting Allie to bed that night, he let his thoughts go to Monica again and texted her: *Almost time! I'm excited!* She texted back immediately: *Me too!*

He went to sleep, thinking of her.

# CHAPTER 13

Matthew, asleep, was awakened when he suddenly heard Allie groaning. Glancing at the bedside clock, he saw it was 1:30 a.m., so he went over to Allie's bed.

"I don't feel good," she said.

He turned on the light to see she looked pale and weak. He touched her forehead, and it was burning.

"My knee hurts," she said.

He took her covers off and slowly peeled off her bandage as she moaned in pain. Her knee was red and swollen and there looked to be a yellowish pus in the center.

His heart began beating quickly, but he needed to remain calm so as not to scare her.

"Okay, we just need to get you some medicine from the doctor."

"My doctor's not here," she said as she started to cry.

"It's okay, it's okay, they have really good other doctors here. I promise you'll feel better once we get you medicine."

He didn't know if that was true. He wanted to cry himself. Her fever had to be really high for her to be that hot. His brain screamed, *Remain calm! Remain calm! Remain calm!*

He picked her up and carried her out to the car, putting her in the passenger seat. Then he Googled "Copenhagen hospitals." There was one called Gentofte two and a half miles away. He hoped GPS would lead him there easily as he drove off.

As much as he wanted to speed, he couldn't be reckless and risk getting into an accident or missing a turn, which would delay things further.

Allie had stopped crying, and he wondered if she felt too ill to do so, as she seemed mostly lethargic now. He turned on the radio hoping music would help soothe her.

"Do you want to sing?" he asked, noticing that it was hard for him to speak with his heart beating so fast.

She shook her head no with little energy. He didn't want to try either because she might panic if she heard him breathing heavily from nerves.

The hospital emergency room had a full crowd, but they managed to take Allie in quickly, recognizing her high temperature. Thankfully, everyone spoke English, which was one of his pros when deciding on the trip. Monica had told him Danes were taught English from a very young age, and 86% of them spoke it as a second language.

Matthew accompanied Allie to her room and sat beside her as she lay on a bed. A nurse began preparing an IV.

"We're going to start getting medicine in you, sweetie," the nurse said.

Matthew held Allie's hand as the nurse prepared to inject the needle and IV into her.

"You'll only feel a little pain prick, and then it'll start working," Matthew said.

The nurse gently inserted the IV and Allie scrunched her face, anticipating the pain. The nurse took out the needle and Allie unscrunched.

"You try to get some rest, okay?" the nurse said to Allie. "A doctor will come in soon to see you." She gave Matthew a reassuring smile and left.

Matthew looked at Allie. She looked pale and weak. His heart was being torn to shreds, but he couldn't show it. He just smiled at her while never feeling more helpless.

"You'll be feeling better soon, okay?"

Did she believe him? Was he hiding his panic? She nodded, so he hoped that meant she believed him.

A doctor, a friendly-looking man who looked to be in his early 60s, came in and examined Allie.

"It's definitely infected," he said. "Let's clean it and get her a fresh bandage." Using a saline solution and a rag, he gently started cleaning her knee—but she cried from the pain as she squeezed Matthew's hand hard.

"You're doing good; it's almost clean," Matthew said.

The doctor finished and applied ointment and then a big bandage on her knee.

"She should try to sleep now," the doctor said to Matthew. "We can talk outside for a minute."

"Can you try and get back to sleep?" Matthew said to Allie.

She nodded yes and closed her eyes.

Matthew and the doctor went outside the room.

"It's a pretty bad infection," the doctor said. "Does she have low immunity?"

"She was born with bronchopulmonary dysplasia. They told me it could affect her immunity."

The doctor nodded. "We'll see if the antibiotics bring her fever down. If she's not responding, we may have to perform a debridement procedure to remove the infected material."

"Is that like a surgery?"

"In a way. We have to cut out the dead tissue. And we'd have to give her anesthesia as it'll be painful."

"Is this something serious?" Matthew said, exhaling deeply.

"Usually, the antibiotics work—and especially the debridement if needed. Her low immunity is a little concerning, though. We'll monitor her very carefully."

Matthew nodded solemnly.

"It's going to be a long night. Would you like a cot for the room?"

"Yes, please."

The doctor nodded and asked a nearby nurse to get a cot for the room.

Matthew went back into Allie's room to see she had her eyes closed. But she opened them when she heard noise. He sat by her. "They're bringing me a bed, so we'll both sleep in here tonight, okay."

Allie nodded and closed her eyes again.

Matthew tried to gather his thoughts as he waited for the cot to come in. His nightmare scenario had come true. He clenched his teeth, urging himself to stay strong.

The cot arrived, but Matthew stayed sitting next to Allie. He'd only go to sleep when his eyes couldn't stay awake anymore.

When Allie finally fell asleep, Matthew paced the room quietly. His stomach and head were hurting. But it was immaterial. He'd trade any kind of pain for her to be better.

Then he remembered Monica was supposed to visit in two days, so he texted her to let her know what had happened.

It was about 6:00 am when Monica texted back how awful she felt for Allie. He texted that he'd call her in a minute. Satisfied that Allie was still asleep, he went into the hallway and called Monica.

"Hey, how is she?"

"I don't know yet. She's sleeping right now, though."

"I'm so sorry for this."

"Yeah. They don't know if she'll get better or worse overnight." He exhaled heavily. "How is this happening?"

"You have to stay positive, Matty. She needs that from you."

"I know. It's just tough."

"I'll let you go. Get some rest while she's sleeping. And give her my best."

"I will. As for you, though…" He trailed off, not knowing how to address her upcoming visit.

"All your focus needs to be on her. Don't worry about me."

"Do you still want to come?"

"If you want me to, I will. If I can be helpful in some way."

He didn't answer immediately, realizing he didn't want her to. "I can't ask that of you. I'll be by her bedside the whole time."

"Of course. That's where you need to be."

"If you can't get a refund, I'll pay for your ticket."

"Don't even think about it. I know how to deal with airlines."

"Okay. Thanks. I'll keep you updated."

"Stay strong. And we'll … see each other when we see each other."

"Yeah."

When they hung up, he went back to Allie's room. She was sleeping. He looked at her, wishing with all he had that she was healing.

Then he thought of his conversation with Monica. He had so looked forward to seeing her, but as he continued watching Allie, nothing mattered but her being well. He wanted all of his thoughts to remain on that.

He stayed by her bedside until he couldn't keep his eyes open any longer. Getting onto his cot, he quickly fell asleep.

\* \* \*

The next few days were just as difficult. Allie's fever would go down and then back up again. The doctor performed the debridement and believed it would help, but he couldn't say for sure.

Watching her struggle with this, without being able to help, was the most difficult thing he'd ever experienced. The only thing that gave him a tiny moment of joy was whenever she'd wake up and see him there, she'd smile.

And during her awake moments, he wanted to keep her mind busy. They'd read together, do puzzles, and play simple card games like War and Go Fish. He had mazes and word searches printed out, so she'd always have one of them to do if needed.

Despite these activities, it felt like time moved glacially. When she was sleeping, he'd walk, eat a little in the cafeteria, and then go back to the room and watch her or doze himself.

One time, after her fever went up again and she cried from not feeling well, he soothed her as best he could until she finally fell back asleep. But he couldn't contain his emotions anymore. He went into the bathroom in her room and sobbed, hoping the fan was loud enough so that she wouldn't be wakened by him. He finally calmed himself down and kept repeating, "She's going to be okay."

With a deep breath, he went back to her side where she was still sleeping. He just watched her while whispering, "You're going to be okay."

\*   \*   \*

On day three, Allie's fever subsided. But would it stay down this time? They'd have to wait and see.

Time continued to move so slowly. Especially when she slept. It was agonizing how slow it was. But he wouldn't move by her bedside.

When she awoke, another good sign. She was hungry. Matthew looked at the nurse, hoping for confirmation that it was a good sign. The nurse gave a small smile and nod, then left and came back with apple sauce.

But the doctor said, "Still too early to tell."

Allie fell asleep again. Matthew stayed and waited.

He didn't mean to, but he fell asleep in the bedside chair. The doctor woke him, gave him a thumbs up, and smiled. Allie was also awake, eating toast. The color had come back to her face, and she had more energy.

"My fever's gone," she said while chewing.

Matthew smiled ear to ear. The relief he felt was enormous.

"Your little fighter's going to be okay," the doctor said.

Matthew effusively thanked him and the nurses, who he'd gotten to know fairly well. He'd be getting them all gifts.

He hugged and kissed Allie and said, "Guess who gets to get out of here?"

With a big smile she said, "Me." He nodded and hugged and kissed her again.

As they waited for the paperwork to discharge her, Matthew and Allie sat by a window in her hospital room and watched a beautiful sunset.

"Sunset's the opposite of sunrise because it sets in the west," he said. "It's my favorite. I love how it makes the sky so colorful—and each time it could be different colors."

"I liked the sunrise," Allie said.

"What'd you like about it?"

"It made the sky orange," she answered. "And I like oranges. And it made me feel warm."

"I like that," he said. "Are you excited about going home?"

"Kinda'. Can I meet Monica another time?"

"Yeah," he said. "Just don't know when. For now, it's just you and me, kiddo."

He didn't know if there'd be a romantic future with Monica. He was still open to it, but it didn't feel as important anymore.

The little girl on his lap was what was important. The life they would lead together was what was important. If Monica ever wanted to come to them, and have a life with them, that would be wonderful. But that would have to be her decision. He wouldn't try forcing it.

He kissed Allie on the head, and they watched the sunset as it went down. He was looking forward to getting home.

# CHAPTER 14

The next few years went by unremarkably. Allie continued to be small for her age and Dr. Bauer said she'd probably always be on the shorter side, possibly under five feet.

But all that Matthew cared about was the person she had become. Sweet, kind and caring. Definitely still an introvert with anxiety issues, though.

When she was seven, she fell off her bike and badly scraped the same knee. That night, he couldn't sleep, checking on her every thirty minutes to make sure she was okay.

Thankfully, it didn't get infected. And overall, her health was in good shape. Especially her lungs, which by every measurement were doing great. The doctor said she should have no limitations there.

She wouldn't ride the bike again, though. The fear of falling again scared her too much. He didn't push, but he hoped she'd get back on the proverbial, and literal, bike one day.

What he was especially excited by was her interest in photography. It had blossomed to where it was her main hobby. As soon as they got home from Denmark, all she wanted to do was take photos. Matthew would show her tricks of the trade, but she also had a natural talent for it.

He bought her first real camera when she was nine. A Nikon D3500 for $350. He wanted her to start with that, and while confident she could handle a more complex camera, because she knew how to use his Sony A1, he thought it best to see how she handled her own first. If she kept at it with seriousness, he'd eventually get her a Sony a7III, which cost $1500.

He and Sherry remained close, but he didn't get to see her as much because her speaking agency was growing, and even though she hired more help, being a hands-on perfectionist meant she was heavily involved. And when she wasn't busy with that, her boys played so many sports—football, basketball, baseball—that she and Kenny were constantly shuttling each one to different practices.

He didn't see Kenny all that often either, but that was more due to Kenny's surliness. When he was in a bad mood, he wasn't fun to be around, and his bad moods increased in frequency. He started coaching some of his boys' teams, but their attitudes and those of their teammates would bother him. He felt they didn't love and respect whatever sport they were playing the way he and his generation did—and if they couldn't, they shouldn't be playing.

It led to a bunch of arguments with Sherry. She'd say, "They're just kids having fun," and he'd counter with, "They don't take it seriously," and she'd counter with, "Your standards are too high." So, he stopped coaching.

When Matthew did see Sherry, it was usually to fit in one of their competitions. She was still better at air hockey and he better at darts.

Both Sherry and Kenny were great with Allie. Every so often, Sherry would take Allie out for a girls' day. He was so appreciative because Allie would get uncomfortable anytime he tried talking to her about female things. And he wasn't entirely comfortable with it either. Plus, he figured Sherry would give much better answers and advice than he would.

The only person Kenny was never grumpy with was Allie. And she loved hearing him talk about his football-playing days.

She started watching Cardinals games on TV with Matthew, and he knew her interest lay in Kenny playing for them. The first time they watched together, he was all she wanted to talk about.

"Did Mr. Kenny make lots of good plays?" Allie asked.

"He did. He was one of the best."

"Which guy was he?"

"The running back. He's the one the quarterback hands the football off to. That's who he was, for most of his career."

"He was someone else sometimes?"

"He was. Let me tell you about Mr. Kenny and how much he loved football. Most of the time when a star running back got older, they got cut from the team—and if they wanted to keep playing they usually had to go to other teams. Or retire. But Mr. Kenny loved playing for the Cardinals so much that he didn't want to leave and was willing to be a backup running back and play special teams. Do you remember who I said were the special teams players?"

"The ones from the beginning of the game?" she asked.

"That's right."

His boss, Phil, visited one day during a Cardinals game and Allie told him when Mr. Kenny played special teams, he was called a gunner, and he'd run down the sideline as fast as possible to tackle the kick or punt returner.

Phil was impressed with her knowledge.

Most of her time growing up felt normal until they hit another rough patch at thirteen when one of her earliest friends, Stephanie, turned on her in the eighth grade. Stephanie made new friends, and Allie didn't fit in with them, so not only did she abandon Allie, but she also got mean. Stephanie teased her in front of others, told secrets about who she had crushes on, just plain meanness.

Matthew talked to her principal, which resulted in Stephanie just ignoring Allie instead of bullying her.

Being such a sensitive kid, it hit Allie hard. Matthew would do his best to be there for her when she was upset, but he didn't feel fully equipped, so she resumed regular therapy.

Before that, starting when she was six, she would only sporadically see her original therapist because no one felt she needed it that much.

As for Monica, they stayed true to their once-a-month video chats. And their friendship blossomed. But it was solely friendship. After the Denmark trip, part of him hoped Monica would come to visit so they could see if the dynamic worked. But she never suggested it. Her life remained the same, still moving to a different country every six months, loving that experience. He knew and expected she knew, too, that a romantic relationship would only work if she moved to Arizona. She didn't. And he became fine with it, enjoying being her friend.

If she had any kind of romantic life, she didn't discuss it, and he never asked. And she never asked if he had a dating life. He didn't, which she probably sensed. He thought he might at some point, but it never seemed to be enough of a desire to pursue it. It was always the same impediment. They wouldn't be Monica. He knew that wasn't rational because so many found new love once they put themselves out there again—but he just didn't want to. And he had a favorite part of his life that gave him all he needed— being Allie's father. Getting to see her grow up was the thrill of his life.

# PART 3

# CHAPTER 15

Allie, now fourteen, sat in her room looking through her camera file folder of sunsets, sunrises, butterflies, birds, flowers and fauna.

Her room was neat and tidy, although decorated minimally. She kept the light purple color scheme, liking that it was her father's choice. Her shelves had plenty of books, mostly nonfiction ones about places in the world, animals, and historical figures that she found inspiring, like Harriet Tubman, Amelia Earhart and Gandhi.

And on a top shelf sat the two urns, the ashes of her real mother and father. Her dad told her they could put the urns anywhere else if she wanted, but having them in her room was meaningful. She never knew them, but she was on earth because of them. She actually didn't think about the urns all that much anymore as they'd been a part of her room for so long.

Her favorite possession was her Sony a7III camera, which currently sat on a tripod in the corner.

Photography was everything to her. She loved capturing images and challenging herself to frame them in unique ways. Like her father, nature shots were her favorite. But she also liked architecture and would take shots of buildings all over town, including her school. Photography never bored her.

Her father knocked on her half-open door. "Let's eat out tonight," he said. "I'm feeling cooped up."

"Do we have to?" Allie asked, staying focused on the photos.

"We're low on food."

"We have Pop Tarts."

"You don't even like the frosted cherry ones," he said as he sat on her bed. "And I'm beholden to make sure you have a certain amount of Riboflavin in every meal."

"We can order in. I'll get the Riboflavin special."

"C'mon, Al. Being amongst other humans is necessary at times. It's healthy."

"I'm amongst humans all day at school," she said. "And a lot of 'em suck."

She was a freshman in high school, and it was a big adjustment from her smaller middle school. There were more cliques, and the halls and cafeteria were louder, rowdier and more intimidating. And she acutely felt how much younger she looked than everyone else.

"Teenagers aren't human," he joked. "They're just pinballing hormones stuffed inside meat suits."

"I'm a teenager," she said, chuckling slightly.

He made pinball sounds and motioned the ball bouncing around.

"Fine, but when you're old and want me to feed you pudding, I'm going to remember you called me a hormonal meat suit."

"Just remember to do the sound effects."

He left, making the pinball sounds again, which made her shake her head and chuckle again.

She went to her floor-length mirror and looked herself over, wondering how much taller than her four-foot-nine height would she grow. She was the shortest among her peers and she thought about it way too much.

Taking a comb to her light brown hair to try to make it less frizzy ended in frustration, as it usually did.

She hated the frizz, but it wasn't that long ago that she never really thought about it. It was only when a former friend of hers from middle school, Stephanie, walked by while she was at her locker and said, "Ever heard of conditioner?" And as she walked off, she said laughing, "Got a head full of frizz."

It had always been a shock to Allie, even going back to elementary school, that others could be so easily judgmental. And then cruel about it.

"I'll be in the car, Al!" her dad yelled from downstairs.

Allie shook her head at herself in the mirror, grabbed her purse, and headed out.

\* \* \*

Matthew and Allie ate at the Olive Garden. He was a fettuccine Alfredo guy and she usually got chicken parmigiana or cheese ravioli—although she just went for basic spaghetti and meatballs this time.

He noticed Allie was a little quiet, which often meant she had a bunch of thoughts twirling in her head. He found that she'd eventually open up if he could get her talking about something. She'd become much more internal lately, though.

They never fought or got angry with each other, but sometimes she could be obstinate. Those moments usually came when she was in the mood she was in now.

Sherry once said to him that their kids' teenage years were like white water rafting for the parent—you just hold on for dear life and hope everyone gets through it okay. And sometimes, it did feel like that.

"Is Stephanie still being a pain?" Matthew asked.

"I don't want to talk about her," she said as she picked at her spaghetti.

He wished he could get her to talk more about Stephanie and what was going on at school. He really wanted to know, but either she didn't want him to know too much, which was worrying, or it was a subject that pained her and so she preferred not to have to deal with it. At least with him.

"Okay," he said. "Have you given any more thought about joining something?"

She only had one friend, Becca, and so he thought if she just joined a group or club, she'd meet new people and gain some confidence. One of her teachers once told him that even if Allie knew the answers she'd never raise her hand—and actually appeared fearful if the teacher looked like she'd call on her. Would joining a group or club help with things like that? He didn't know, but it couldn't hurt. She rarely wanted to talk about it, though.

And this time was no different as she gave a little no head shake.

At least she had Becca. They had met the summer before high school when Becca's mom took her to a gallery event that featured some of Matthew's photos. They hit it off instantly, as Becca had similar experiences with being bullied at her middle school. But they'd be going to the same high school, if Allie chose to go.

After her rough eighth-grade experience with Stephanie, Allie had asked if she could be home-schooled moving forward.

He said yes, but if she was, he did want her to join a group or club outside of school hours. She was hesitant and uncomfortable with meeting a whole new set of people, so she asked to think about it more.

But now that Becca would be going to school, she changed her mind. And he was happy about that, not just because she had a close friend but also because he thought being around many new kids in high school would be best for her development. At least that was the hope.

He pressed on, "I just—"

"Want me to be happy, I know," she said, cutting him off. "I talk about these things in therapy."

"Fair enough," he said. "But I really believe you might make more friends."

"Dad."

He held his hands up in an 'okay, no more' way.

Allie looked at a woman standing by herself at the bar. "For making me come here I'm thinking of going up to her and saying, 'My dad's single, please be my mommy?'"

He laughed. "Could little Miss Shyness ever be that bold?"

"If embarrassing you is on the line I might be."

"Let's not test it out then."

"It could be everlasting love," she teased.

"You're killing me, Al," he said, chuckling.

He knew it was her subtle way of reminding him he didn't like talking about certain things either.

He still had chosen not to date. And he was completely okay with that—never once feeling he was denying himself something. Allie was his main priority. That was his choice. In no way was it forced.

But Sherry felt it was. She believed his reasoning was he didn't want to risk disrupting Allie's life in a negative way, especially now during the tougher teen years. And that was true. But he'd tell her two things could be true, and the other true thing was he just didn't want to date. That might change one day, but not now.

He did wonder if Monica lived in Arizona, would he date her? Probably. He knew that was a complete contradiction, but he also knew Monica intimately, and Allie had gotten to know her some over the years, too. And he didn't think she'd disrupt Allie's life, and if she did, he'd choose Allie.

Weirdly enough, though, he didn't pine for Monica. Their friendship was still solid, and it'd been a good while now since they dated. What they had, when they had it, was near perfect. Until it wasn't. That was life and he accepted it.

His lack of dating was hard to explain to Allie, so he preferred not to.

He was about to bring up a more pleasant subject for both, where they should go on their next vacation, when he got a text notification from Sherry.

"Sherry sent an 'Ahhhh' with what looks like fifteen exclamation points."

"Oh no. I know that fifteen exclamations feeling."

He motioned for the server to come over while saying to Allie, "We'll bring a dessert."

\*    \*    \*

When Matthew and Allie arrived at Sherry's house, she was in the kitchen, drinking a glass of wine and frazzled. He couldn't remember the last time he saw her drink alcohol. Dirty dishes sat in the sink, another rare thing to see in Sherry's kitchen.

Matthew put the dessert box on the table and opened it for her to see a chocolate truffle cake, her favorite. It made her smile. "You're almost tempting me to have freak-out moments often if this is at the end of the rainbow."

Allie headed straight for the pile of dishes and started washing them. It made Sherry smile again. "How'd a blockhead like you raise such an angel?"

Matthew laughed. "Got lucky," he said as he helped Allie with the dishes.

"I'm sorry I got you guys here," Sherry said. "With Kenny in one of his big funks I'm just..." she trailed off.

Kenny had become more surly and distant. He hung out less with Matthew or any of his old teammates or friends, and when he wasn't giving a speech that Sherry set up, he would sit in their basement and watch TV or go to a bar and just sit by himself and drink.

Matthew engaged with him when he could, but Kenny seemed to be in a bad mood more times than not. Seeing him this way was difficult, especially because he had no idea how to help him.

"We gotta try to get him to see someone," Matthew said.

"So proud of his damn toughness when he played," Sherry said. "Never needed help. I tell him these funks aren't high ankle sprains."

Her son, Darius, now 16 and with his father's athletic build, only a little stockier, walked in, eyeballing the cake. "Ooh, can I have some?"

"No," Sherry said, then softened. "All right, get a plate. Only 'cause dealing with your game schedules is one of the things that led to them bringing this."

Darius brought his plate over. "I should stress you out more, then," he joked.

"Boy, don't play with me," she said, holding in a laugh. "And you should be doing the dishes, not them."

Darius took the cake and started eating while saying to Matthew and Allie, "You guys are doing great. Keep it up."

They both started splashing him with bubbles as he sprinted out before they got him.

Sherry's kids were still like brothers to Allie, but she didn't get to see them as much because they were so busy with the various sports they played and went to private schools. NFL money could afford that. He wished they went to Allie's school because they'd look after her. But that wasn't how it was, so he didn't dwell on it much.

However, they still treated her like a sister whenever they saw her, which he and Allie appreciated.

Sherry enjoyed the interplay, and he could see she was de-stressing some. She got up and hugged them both. "Thank you."

"If you'd adopt us, we could move in and be helpful like this more," Matthew joked.

"Allie can stay," Sherry said. "There's enough boys here already."

*    *    *

Her dad left to check on Kenny in the basement, so Allie sat with Sherry.

"I would have paid anything to see you go up to that woman and say that," Sherry said, chuckling.

"We all know I never could," Allie said.

"Yeah, but if you did, make sure I'm there next time. Or at least record it."

Allie laughed. She was so grateful she had Sherry in her life. Entering her teen years, there were certain things she had a harder time talking about with her father, especially the female stuff. It was kind of embarrassing. And she thought it made him a little squeamish as well.

But she could talk about them with Sherry, and she always had answers. And not just with female issues, but anything. And she couldn't have admired someone more. Running a successful business while raising three kids. And confident. It's something they talked about quite a bit. How to be confident? Sherry would say, "You have to believe in yourself because if you don't, no one else will."

And Allie would ask how someone could actually do that. Sherry would say, "You just do it. You just believe and don't question it."

Not that easy for Allie, though. She'd dealt with anxiety her whole life. It was a part of who she was as a person. And while she could generate confidence about being a photographer, she felt she was lacking in every other way.

Sherry, Allie's therapist Patricia, and her dad would tell her it'd get easier as she got older. She hoped they were right.

"He knows you feel guilty about him not having a dating life," Sherry said.

"Yeah. I mean he can say it's not because of me, but of course I'm a big reason why."

"It's more complicated than that. But I agree you shouldn't feel guilty. It's on him."

"Can guilt be controlled?"

"Everything can be controlled. At least in theory."

"It'd be a whole lot easier if he actually started dating," Allie said, laughing.

"I'm working on him, honey. I think I'm wearing him down."

"Maybe that woman's still at the restaurant," Allie said, smiling. "Should we go back and check?"

"So tempting," Sherry said, laughing.

She wished she didn't feel guilty over her dad being single. But he prioritized her, and she was so grateful for it, but how could she not believe he wasn't sacrificing his happiness in some way?

There was nothing she could do about it, though, except tell him she would be okay with him trying to find love and wanted it for him. He'd just smile, give her a hug, and say he was happy. She hoped he was truthful because she wanted him to be happy.

\*   \*   \*

Matthew went down the basement stairs to see Kenny sitting on the couch, zoned out. It was a large basement with pool and ping-pong tables and three TVs. Plus, several framed action photos of Kenny from his playing days in college and the NFL—all shot by Matthew. And in a corner sat a case with trophies Kenny won for Rookie of the Year, Offensive Player of the Year and Walter Payton Man of the Year.

Matthew sat next to Kenny, who didn't look at him. They said nothing for a while. Finally, Kenny said, "Remember when you used to come over to see me?"

Matthew didn't respond as they continued to sit in silence. During Kenny's playing days, he, Kenny and friends spent a lot of time in the basement. Watching sports, talking trash, downing beers, playing ping-pong or pool. Great times. But without a bunch of people there, it had a lonely feeling.

"Sherry probably asked, and you ran right over."

Matthew again didn't respond. He didn't want to argue. After more silence, he finally said, "You're struggling with something, K. For a while now."

Kenny put his hand up, not wanting to talk about it. Matthew nodded okay.

Kenny still hadn't replaced playing football with anything that could remotely give him the same fulfillment. And he stopped trying. Matthew's old boss with the Cardinals told him Kenny even turned down offers to be on the coaching staff or part of the broadcast team.

"Let's get a drink sometime," Matthew said.

"No, no. No charity."

They sat in more silence. Matthew finally got up. "I'm here if you need me."

Kenny said nothing. Matthew left. It was an empty feeling, but he didn't know how to fix things. Mental health manifested itself differently in everyone. And when someone wouldn't seek help or even acknowledge they might need help, there was very little anyone could do about it. Kenny was one of the toughest dudes to ever play football. He wore it as a badge of honor. And to him, tough dudes didn't need help.

Matthew also felt horrible for Sherry because she needed Kenny, and she loved him.

# CHAPTER 16

Allie hated the cafeteria at her school. It made her the most anxious because so many of her fellow students were there, in their friend or clique group. And it was always loud. An obnoxious kind of loud. And today wasn't any different.

Every time she did this walk with her tray of food and milk carton past tables of boisterous students, it felt like a mile. And she felt like a robot, stiff and a little slow. She wondered if anyone analyzed how she walked, and if so, would they make fun of her for it? She hated thinking like that and yet she couldn't stop herself.

And then her nightmare happened. She misstepped a little, enough to make her lose her solid grip on the tray. The milk carton tumbled over and splatted on the ground.

She froze as all eyes went to her. The boisterous ones did what boisterous ones do. Laughing. Pointing. Cackling.

All she could think about was getting away as quickly as possible, so Allie started walking on when one of the boisterous ones said, "Ain't you gonna pick it up?"

Allie froze again, making it more noticeable. Then she turned back to the milk carton, bending to pick it up when her food plate slipped off her tray and hit the ground.

The boisterous ones really had a field day as their phones came out to record.

She picked it all up as quickly as she could and walked off briskly to where her friend Becca sat at a table by herself.

When she sat, she fought back tears, and Becca put her arm around her.

"I swear I'm going to punch one of them one day," Becca said.

Becca was like Allie in that she didn't have other friends. While they were opposites in appearance, with Becca facing a lot of teasing due to her size and weight, she handled it differently. She was feisty. She stood up for herself. Allie wished she had Becca's verve. And Becca loved Allie's kindness. They spent as much time together as possible.

Becca noticed that some girls were looking at them and laughing from a few tables down.

"Surprise, surprise, your former bitch friend thought it was funny," Becca said.

Allie looked up to see one of the girls, Stephanie, was leading the laughs.

Most of her time growing up felt normal, until Stephanie turned on her in the eighth grade. And she'd only gotten meaner since.

Once, when passing her in the hall, she pushed Allie into her locker. And she'd often look at Allie, say something to her friends, and they'd all start laughing. It's how she was when she first got mean back in eighth grade and now renewed it in high school. Allie thought it was Stephanie's way of marking her territory in a new place.

And she knew her dad wanted her to talk about Stephanie, but she believed if she told him the bullying restarted, it would make things worse for her. When Stephanie started bullying her in eighth grade, her dad did talk to the principal. And it worked; Stephanie went from bullying to just ignoring—but everyone knew her father had intervened, and her peers treated her like some sort of snitch. And no one wanted to be friends with a snitch.

If it weren't for Becca, there was no way she'd want to go to high school. She made it bearable.

"She'd be the first one I'd punch," Becca said, glaring at Stephanie.

"You'll just get in trouble."

"Don't care," Becca said. "I hate this place, except for you... You okay?"

Allie wasn't but said, "Yeah."

"If you wanted to go on a diet there was a better way."

Allie laughed a little, and Becca hugged her. "C'mon, let's get you another lunch."

Other than her father and Sherry, Becca had become the most important person in her life. Being able to talk with someone her age who had shared experiences meant everything.

The fact that cliques even existed fascinated and disappointed them. They knew from their parents that cliques were a part of high school for as long as anyone could remember. How teens didn't evolve out of falling into groups baffled her. She, of course, wasn't even in a clique unless being a nobody was a category.

She wasn't interested in being one of the popular kids, but she sometimes wondered what being extroverted would be like. They seemed like they were having more fun. But were they just as scared as her and hid it behind a gregarious, outgoing personality? She'd like to think they were, just to feel more equal. In the end, it didn't matter. She was who she was, and she couldn't change it.

"My father's still bugging me about joining something," Allie said as she and Becca headed to the food area.

"If he saw all the annoying people at this school, he might drop it."

"He doesn't believe they're all annoying. He thinks there's gotta be another you here."

"Could anyone possibly be that fabulous?" Becca said, chuckling.

"Impossible," Allie said, chuckling also.

Allie knew there could be others she'd get along with, but she hadn't met any yet, and she definitely met so many she didn't want to be around. And that was enough to keep her from joining anything.

Allie and Becca headed back to their table after getting her a new lunch, and as they passed by Stephanie's table, she glanced to see Stephanie staring at her intently with an impish smile, as if hoping Allie would drop her tray again.

She didn't. And this cafeteria session would soon be over. But later that day, she had the one thing she may have hated more than the cafeteria. Gym class.

# CHAPTER 17

"I'm loving how uncomfortable you are," Sherry said as she and Matthew walked in the mall. He carried a tablet.

"Really? I hadn't noticed," Matthew said, chuckling.

"That first time I met you, I said to myself, 'One day I'm gonna be taking this dude to learn about training bras,'" she said, laughing.

Matthew laughed as well while shaking his head at her enjoyment. He didn't like that learning about the right bras and feminine hygiene products for Allie made him uncomfortable. It shouldn't. He was her parent. But it did. And he could tell it made Allie uncomfortable, too. And maybe that's why he was uncomfortable.

And it was also another reminder that his little girl was growing up. But since she was small and looked so young it was hard to wrap his head around it. And at times like these it felt like it was happening too fast.

That's what he thought whenever he researched anything about her female needs. And while he did as much learning on the Internet as he could, he needed more knowledge if he was going to buy her the appropriate things for her body. So, going to a bra store was necessary. And he knew Sherry would tease him endlessly, but going with her made it a little more comfortable. Thankfully, she agreed to go.

"I tell Allie it's my fault you don't date 'cause I do stuff like this with you," Sherry said. "If I didn't, you'd be on every dating site."

"What, you think my message to potential dates would be—I'm not interested in love or companionship, just someone to help my daughter buy her bras?"

"I think you'd phrase it better," Sherry said, laughing again.

He knew while she was joking, she was also partly being serious. They actually hadn't talked about his lack of a dating life in a while, but this excursion seemed to reignite the issue.

"I've told you a million times your life revolves too much around her, especially worrying about her," she said. "Her anxiety, not being developed yet, lack of friends. That can't be all your life is."

"I don't think that's accurate. Beating you in darts is also a major part of my life."

"First, don't rile me up, Bullseye Baby. Second, I want you to date so you'll be in a great relationship. Who wouldn't want that?"

"Is 'great' guaranteed?"

"See, that's why Allie feels guilty. You say stuff like that."

"It's a fair question."

"She interprets it to mean it has to be perfect for both of you."

"It kinda' does."

"But you know perfect doesn't exist, so you don't even bother trying."

"Your words, not mine."

"And what are your words?" she asked.

"You gotta let life happen," he replied. "Today I'm single. Who knows what tomorrow will bring."

"Tomorrow isn't gonna bring Monica here."

He laughed. "How many times do I have to say I'm not hung up on her? We're friends."

Sherry gave a doubting, "Mm-hm."

They arrived at Janie's Bras. "It's go time. You ready?" she asked.

"I'd rather dunk my head in the fountain."

"You can do that after," Sherry said, chuckling.

They went in. He noticed the mannequins first. Lots of them. All wearing bras and lingerie ranging from sports bras to intricate lace options. The racks and shelves looked as if they were organized by type and size, and size charts were displayed on the walls, which had a lot more letters and numbers than Matthew expected. Pinks and pastels abounded, and the varied scents of perfumes were undeniable.

As they walked around, Matthew noticed the women shopping were looking at them out of curiosity. It made him even more uncomfortable, which Sherry noticed.

"Is that dating site looking better?" she asked.

He chose not to respond.

*   *   *

Matthew and Sherry stood with a saleswoman who looked to be in her mid-thirties and dressed professionally in a black skirt and blazer with a white top. She showed a hint of surprise when she first saw him but recovered quickly.

"Since he refuses to find a partner or even try, he's here to learn about his daughter's bra needs before he shops with her," Sherry said.

"Ignore the first part. But I am here to learn options for my daughter. She's fourteen and it'll be her first bra."

"What's her body type?" the saleswoman asked.

"Small. Uh, less developed."

"Okay, I can show you some options."

Matthew and Sherry followed the saleswoman to an area near the back of the store. "And he's going to write down every word of info you give," Sherry said.

They arrived at a section of training bras, and Sherry pointed at Matthew to get ready to write. He opened a new document on the tablet and took out a Stylus pen from his pocket.

Sherry noticed more women looking at them with curiosity, and she turned to announce, "He's single, ladies. I'll hand out his card when we're done."

Matthew could only chuckle as he blushed and shook his head at her. Then, to the saleswoman, "Please proceed."

"It'll be her preference when she tries some on—but there are many types of training bras," the saleswoman said. "Since you're in learning mode, a training bra does not actually train the breasts."

"Start writing," Sherry instructed him, which he did on the tablet.

The saleswoman continued, "Its main purpose is to provide a bit of camouflage, protection and support for tender breast buds and nipples."

"That's right. Keep writing," Sherry said.

Matthew kept writing as the saleswoman showed him a bra. "A seamless bralette like this has a versatile J-clip that allows it to be worn as a racerback, which is the straps resting between the shoulder blades in an X shape."

Matthew kept writing as the saleswoman showed them another bra.

"Or this with spaghetti straps is more discreet."

"Did you get all that down?" Sherry asked him.

"Uh-huh," he said.

"Let me see," Sherry said, taking the tablet.

She saw all he wrote over and over was, "I'M IN HELL!!!!!!!!"

Sherry shot him a look while the saleswoman, who also saw it, chuckled.

"Is that not what you said?" Matthew said jokingly to the saleswoman.

Sherry fought a laugh as she shook her head at him.

"I actually learned a bit of what you said Online already," Matthew said. "But it's helped to have you confirm it."

As they left the store, Matthew exhaled with a bit of relief.

"You can go dunk your head in the fountain now."

"No thanks. You've had enough enjoyment at my expense already."

"Girl's gotta have fun somehow," she responded.

"It will be easier now when I take Allie back to buy one of 'em."

"Stop it. You know I'm going to take her."

"Oh, thank God."

"But I'm only doing it because it'd be hell for her to shop there with you."

"I guess I owe you again."

"We're up past a million IOUs by now."

"But who's counting?"

They laughed and headed back to the parking lot. He hadn't actually known Sherry would offer to shop with Allie. He believed her when she'd say if he was going to be both the mom and dad, he'd have to get used to doing mom stuff. And he would. But he'd be forever grateful for anything she was willing to help with.

And he knew Allie would be relieved.

As he thought of her, he realized it was the time of day for her gym class, which she made clear was not her favorite. She never said why, but he surmised it probably had something to do with her size and lack of development. He hoped today's session wouldn't be too bad for her.

# CHAPTER 18

"I so don't want to run today," Becca said as she and Allie changed into their gym clothes in the girls' locker room. They both opted for baggy shorts and long, loose-fitting T-Shirts.

"How many have you think tried limping?" Allie joked. She then mimicked a little fake limp. "I want to run, Ms. Donald, but my ankle."

"I'd probably forget which ankle I fake injured," Becca said, laughing.

Becca always started a conversation when they had to change into their gym clothes because she knew how self-conscious Allie was about it. And Allie appreciated it, because it did help distract her. Still, she couldn't wait to not be in the gym locker room as her lack of body development stood out the most here. Nothing else made her feel more different. The looks she'd get, and the occasional snicker, were like daggers.

She once went into a bathroom stall to change, but several looked at her as she exited with knowing looks, and of course, Stephanie and her friends noticed and snickered about it.

"Since your dad has connections with the Cardinals, maybe he can get us one of their trainers to give us a private gym class."

"We could say we're training for football. Who wouldn't believe us?"

"Exactly. We're supreme athletes. I can almost do one whole pushup."

"So impressive," Allie said as they laughed.

She thought it was a shame she had such a negative connotation with gym class because she liked some sports. And she enjoyed watching the Cardinals play on TV with her dad. She had been a fan for as long as she could remember, and especially because it was the team Kenny played for. She wished she got to see him play. He told the best stories about his playing days, and she so admired his passion for it. She had that same passion for photography. And she understood why he dealt with sadness over not getting to do it anymore. If someone told her she couldn't take pictures anymore, it would break her heart.

"Does your dad still yell at the TV during games?"

"Yep," Allie said, laughing. "If the referee makes a bad pass interference call, he goes crazy. It's really funny."

"You should record it and put it on social. It could go viral."

"He would kill me."

Becca then noticed that Stephanie and her friends were looking in their direction and laughing from across the locker room.

Allie looked over and said, "Ignore her."

Stephanie and her friends laughed even harder. Allie could see Becca was not going to ignore her.

"Is something funny?" Becca yelled over to them.

"What's it to you?" Stephanie said back.

"If you want to say something, say it to my face," Becca said.

"Shut up," Stephanie replied.

"You laugh 'til you're called out, and then you become a wuss," Becca said with a dismissive wave.

"You know no one likes you, right?" Stephanie said, and then motioned to Allie, "And she doesn't count, 'cause she's like a ten-year-old."

"And you're a bitch," Becca said.

"You want to know what I said," Stephanie replied. "You've got huge gross saggy mountains and she's flat as a pancake ... if they combined you two, you'd be normal."

Becca started charging her when the gym teacher, Ms. Donald, a fit woman in her 50s, rushed in and got in Becca's way.

"No, no, no, Ms. Carlson," Ms. Donald said. "You need to calm down."

Stephanie and her friends walked off laughing as Stephanie mimed Becca's chest size.

"Look at her," Becca said. Stephanie stopped her mimicking just as Ms. Donald turned to look.

"I'll deal with her," Ms. Donald said. "But you need to get ahold of your emotions."

Ms. Donald walked off after Stephanie and her friends. Allie knew Ms. Donald would, at best, do the absolute minimum. Stephanie ran track. She was popular. Ms. Donald had seen her be crappy to others before and had done nothing about it.

Thank God Allie had Becca; otherwise, she wouldn't have known how to cope with being at school.

# CHAPTER 19

"Kenny!" Sherry yelled as she and Matthew walked into her kitchen. They saw unwashed pans were on the stove, dirty dishes in the sink, and sauce stains splattering the counter.

"What?" Kenny yelled back from another room.

"The kitchen!"

After a few moments, Kenny walked in. Upon seeing Matthew, his mood turned sour.

"I did some cookin'," Kenny said. "I wanted to play pickleball but our fourth was busy." He made sure to look at Matthew.

"You never said you needed a fourth," Matthew said. "Just asked if I could play."

"I was helping him with something for Allie," Sherry said. "But none of that explains this mess."

"Said you were here for me," Kenny said to Matthew, then turned to Sherry. "Your buddy can help you clean it." With that, he left. All Sherry could do was sigh.

"So, today's an angry Kenny day," Matthew said.

"The angry days outnumbering the non, lately," she replied.

Matthew motioned to the dishes. "You want help with this?"

"No, he's doing it," she said stubbornly as she sat with a sigh.

Matthew's phone rang, and a North Carolina area code appeared. Curious, he answered, "Hello."

"Hello, are you related to Allie Russell?" a woman asked.

"Yes, I'm her father."

The woman said she was calling from St. Patrick's Nursing Home and that Allie's grandfather, who had dementia, was in his last days. His wife had died a few years earlier and there was no other family, so they were trying to track Allie down.

"Allie's never met her grandparents," he said. "Which was their choice."

"He's bequeathing what he owns, which is very little, to his church, but we thought there might be belongings that Allie may want."

"I'll have to get back to you," he said.

They hung up.

"The grandparents that never wanted her have resurfaced?" Sherry asked.

"One's gone. The other's close."

"They want you to go there?"

"If Allie wants any belongings."

"She might. You've got spring break coming up."

"She was excited about going to Montana."

"My guess is she'd prefer Carolina now."

"Yeah. I'll let her pick."

He assumed Allie would choose North Carolina and the chance to learn something about her mom. He also thought it might be a sad trip, but he'd leave the choice up to her.

That's something he thought he had gotten better at. Not trying to protect her from everything. Sadness was part of life. She'd experience it sometimes, regardless of what he did.

Like he experienced sadness with his relationship with Kenny. "Should I try to talk to him?"

"Not in the mood he's in."

Matthew didn't know how to fix things, and it became easier to not even try. Kenny was his best friend for so much of his life. Now, he didn't know what they were. Would things change for the better one day? He hoped it would, but they were such different people now.

He knew Kenny's differences took a toll on Sherry, too. His varying moods were difficult for her, but she insisted she was managing.

The last time they had a real conversation about him she admitted things weren't perfect, but believed they'd be okay because he still communicated with her about everything. That was their north star. If he ever stopped communicating, that's when she'd worry.

He hoped for her it would never come to that.

# CHAPTER 20

"That'll be the farthest we're away from each other since we met," Becca said to Allie as they plopped down on Allie's bed.

"I know," Allie said. "It's well over three thousand miles."

Allie was going to North Carolina over spring break, and Becca would be going to Oregon, where her mom had family. When her dad told her about her grandfather, she immediately wanted to go there instead of Montana. The idea of Montana excited her, but the chance to learn something about her mom outweighed everything else. She hadn't really thought about her in years, but her curiosity returned. If she saw where her mom grew up, went to school, or anything, she could learn something, even if it was just a tiny morsel.

"What weird dessert did your dad get us this time?" Becca asked, chuckling.

"I don't know," Allie said. "Maybe it's another Bundt cake."

"Who would name a cake that?"

"Maybe it was invented by a guy named Bundt."

"I so hope that's true."

They both laughed. Since it was Friday, Allie asked her dad if Becca could stay over that night, and he said yes. Sometimes on Fridays Becca stayed over, and sometimes Allie stayed at Becca's. It was a way for them to end another school week on a high note. And this time, they both felt they needed it after the gym locker annoyance.

"Do you think you'll meet people who knew your mom well?"

"My dad kind of warned me we might not meet too many. She wasn't a social butterfly. Like mother like daughter."

"But you might meet some. You never know."

Allie didn't talk too much about her real mom and dad with Becca. Mostly because she didn't know that much. But she had told her they killed themselves right after she was born. It left Becca speechless. Suicide was a heavy topic.

Becca leaned in towards Allie and took a selfie of them as they flashed peace signs with tongues out. Becca looked at the picture. "My eighteen followers must see this."

Allie laughed. "They must."

Becca posted it on her Instagram page with the caption: *Epic* followed by a bunch of silly face emojis.

"I wish you'd post your pics," Becca said. "They're art."

"No, thank you. Last thing I need are Instagram trolls trashing me."

"No one in their right mind would trash you. And if the yearbook people were smart, they'd ask you to take all the pics."

"Ha! Not likely."

"It's only 'cause you're quiet," Becca lamented. "They never try to find the talented, quiet kids. Just the extroverts, whether they have talent or not."

Becca's phone made a notification sound.

"Did someone comment?" Allie asked, leaning in to see Becca's phone. Someone with the handle miz_biz2012 wrote under Becca's post of their selfie: *Two of the ugliest people ever*, followed by sick face emojis.

And then more comments from other accounts came in rapid succession, just as mean:

*The useless twins*

*Embarrassments*

*I hope they choke on fent*

*The fat one's a bitch*

*They actually think they cute*

More and more insults popped up. They sat there, stunned, as they took it all in.

Then Becca got an anonymous text: *You should unalive yourself.*

More mean texts rolled in on her phone in rapid succession.

Becca began to cry and shake. All Allie could do was hold her as she cried as well. She knew this was Stephanie's doing. And it went above her usual meanness. This was cruelty.

\* \* \*

"You're where?" Matthew asked. He was video chatting with Monica while lying on his living room couch with his laptop on his stomach.

"Comoros," Monica replied, motioning to the beautiful scenic background behind her.

"Where is that?"

"Between Madagascar and Mozambique."

"Of course it is."

"It's so beautiful here," she said. "And because dumb-dumbs like you don't know about it, no tourists."

"If I Googled 'great places to travel with no tourists,' wouldn't I find it?"

"Well, Google is for dumb-dumbs."

"You just like making me jealous with these amazing places you go to."

"Guilty," she said. "One of these days you'll give in." Then she smiled in a flirtatious way.

*Whoa, she just flirted with me*, Matthew thought. If a smile could be like a flirty wink, that was it. And it threw him for a second—until he realized he liked it. He smiled back the same way. "Maybe I will."

Neither said anything right away, just continuing to smile at each other. Finally, she said, "I want to see if you still have that belt I bought you all those years ago."

"Why would I ever get rid of such a perfect gift?"

Another few seconds of silence and smiling before she said, "I do have to run. But I'm going to be thinking about that belt."

"I'll polish it up as soon as we say goodbye."

As they signed off, Matthew leaned back, not expecting the flirty turn. They hadn't seen each other in person in fourteen years. He long ago accepted they'd just be friends. And he was perfectly fine with that. But that flirty smile got him. As he kept thinking about it, he reminded himself that their circumstances hadn't changed. Could he do a long-distance romance with her now that Allie was older? He didn't think so. The occasionality of that didn't appeal to him. He'd just be left with wanting more and become frustrated, and he thought she'd probably become frustrated by his wanting more. The only way it'd work was if she came and lived in Arizona. And even that had variables, mainly Allie. She'd always be his priority.

As he thought of Allie, he realized she and Becca hadn't been out of her room all evening. On previous sleepovers, they rarely just stayed in her room, usually having fun in the kitchen making pancakes or cookies and always teasing him about something: how he was dressed, a dessert he bought, a corny joke he would tell. He looked forward to what new way they could rib him.

He headed to Allie's room just to see if everything was all right.

\* \* \*

Allie still held Becca, who had stopped crying but looked defeated.

Her father knocked on her door. "You guy's good in there?" he asked.

Allie took a beat as Becca gave her a 'don't tell him' headshake. Conflicted, Allie replied, "We're good."

\* \* \*

Matthew looked at Allie's door. Something felt off. He lingered, not sure whether to pursue it. It was most likely a teen issue and they probably didn't want him intruding. He respected that, but he didn't like the feeling that something felt off.

Reluctantly, he said, "Come say goodnight before you guys go to sleep, okay."

"Yeah, we will," Allie replied.

Matthew lingered a little longer but then walked off.

\* \* \*

Allie continued comforting Becca, stroking her hair. The moment felt too big for her to handle. If Becca hadn't asked her to keep it between them, she would have told her father something because he had a way of knowing. Probably because she didn't have the best poker face, but he was also very perceptive. So, she assumed he had a feeling that things weren't perfect—and appreciated him not pushing.

She didn't know how to handle this, though. What would school be like? Someone, most likely Stephanie, told Becca she should kill herself. It definitely crossed the line. She thought the principal of her school should be told, or some authority figure, but it was Becca's call. She wouldn't do anything to betray the trust of her best friend. But she hoped Becca would tell either her mom or someone at school.

They didn't talk much the rest of the night and went to bed early.

And all she could think about while trying to fall asleep was how awful school would be on Monday.

\* \* \*

Matthew sat on the living room couch, TV remote in hand. He didn't turn it on yet.

His issue of being a worrier ever since Allie entered his life was rearing its head. He couldn't help himself. Looking up at the ceiling, he sighed.

Allie had come down earlier to say goodnight by herself. He again refrained from asking what was up, but it seemed even more obvious now that things weren't exactly copacetic.

Should he give Becca's mom a heads-up? He'd see how things were in the morning before deciding.

Sitting there, he wondered if he could even think about the moment he and Monica shared. It didn't feel right to, but what if he was overreacting to nothing and denied himself the enjoyment of their flirtation? His brain batted the thoughts of Allie/Becca and Monica back and forth. And the Allie/Becca side won. Something felt off. He hoped he'd learn more the next day.

He got up earlier than usual, so he'd be in the kitchen before Allie and Becca. He assumed Becca would show for that. And she and Allie did. And they acted normally. Maybe they were doing it for show, but all he had to go on was what he could see. And they seemed fine. Even going along with things when he threw dad jokes at them. They did their usual groaning and shaking their heads.

So, he thought maybe it was just a teen moment, and it had passed. He decided not to worry. And with that, he turned his thoughts back to Monica. Would they chat again sooner than usual? Would things turn even flirtier? And what would that mean for them? He chuckled, realizing he hadn't had these kinds of thoughts and feelings in a long time.

# CHAPTER 21

Monday arrived. Allie had a huge pit in her stomach on the bus ride to school. She sat alone in the middle, as she often did, staring out the window. She didn't want to look at anyone and had no idea if anyone was looking at her.

There was quiet chatter like usual, but nothing about her and Becca's situation, at least anything she could hear.

Somehow, the potholes felt even bumpier and more plentiful. But maybe she thought she just was more aware of them because she was more awake than usual.

The weekend had been tough. For the first time that she could remember, she didn't give away that something was amiss to her father. It was so important to Becca not to tell anyone. The morning after the incident, Becca implored her to act as normal as possible. In the kitchen with her father, she could tell his antenna was up. But she and Becca acted normal. In turn, that made him relax and act normal. They even managed to smile and groan at his jokes.

But she didn't like how keeping this from him made her feel. Her mind was so confused by what the right thing to do was, as if it was paralyzed.

She and Becca had talked on the phone throughout the weekend, and at first, Becca spoke quietly, as if the cruelty had crushed her spirit. But once the shock started wearing off, she became angry. That scared Allie a little because Becca was already feisty when pushed. She didn't want her to do anything crazy. Becca said she wouldn't, but if Stephanie or anyone else said anything to her, she wouldn't hold back.

So, Allie didn't know what to expect.

The bus arrived at school. It wasn't too crowded as most were inside already. As she made her way inside and walked the school halls, she now felt eyes were on her. It was the worst kind of attention.

She still didn't want to look at anyone. So as best she could, she kept her eyes on the posters on the walls announcing sports events and club meetings while ensuring she didn't walk into anyone. That was easy to happen as a bunch of kids walked while looking at their phones. And as usual, she had to occasionally dodge someone's backpack from knocking her aside.

She saw Becca at her locker and beelined over. Becca looked tired. Allie rubbed her arm in support.

Before they could even start talking, Stephanie and her friends walked by. "Love your IG," Stephanie said to them.

Allie shot her a furious look. Stephanie just laughed at her, as did her friends.

Allie looked at Becca to see her reaction, but Becca was already on the move as she rushed over and punched Stephanie in the face. Hard.

Stephanie fell and screamed. Becca jumped on top of her and started hitting her more, as Stephanie's friends tried pulling her off and some hitting her as well.

There was screaming and shouts of "Fight!" and "Girl fight!" and people whooping and hollering.

Allie watched it all, shell-shocked. Her body felt literally too paralyzed to move.

A teacher finally rushed in and broke up the fight. Stephanie had gotten the worst of it, as she was crying and bleeding from a cut near the top of her head.

Two teachers walked Becca straight to the principal's office, and another took Stephanie to the nurse's room.

As the commotion in the hallway settled down, Allie couldn't stop shaking. It wasn't a surprise that Becca did what she did, but she still couldn't believe it actually happened.

She rushed to the nearby bathroom, went into a stall and sobbed as quietly as she could. What would happen to Becca? She was sure she'd get the brunt of the discipline despite Stephanie doing the most awful thing. She now wished she had told her dad because maybe the school would have kicked Stephanie out for it. But now, Becca might be the one kicked out of school.

She heard others walking in and out, but she wasn't sure if they could hear her crying. No one asked how she was doing.

The bell rang. Allie wiped her tears, took a deep breath, and went to her first class, social studies, sitting in her back row seat. But she couldn't focus even a little. She just kept replaying the fight in her head over and over. Thankfully, her teacher didn't call on her.

During class breaks, she tried texting Becca but didn't hear back. She figured the principal took her phone away and probably turned it off. After school, she called Becca's mom and found out that the school had suspended Becca. But they were talking expulsion as well.

Becca's mom was furious. She wanted to go to war with the school because it didn't appear that Stephanie was going to be punished. They didn't have proof she sent the *You should unalive yourself* text. Right now, they considered Stephanie the victim.

Allie told her to let Becca know she was there for her. Her mom thanked her and as they hung up, Allie had to fight off tears again.

She thought about calling her dad to pick her up instead of taking the bus, but she just wasn't ready to talk about it. She knew he'd immediately jump into protective mode, but again, she didn't know what that entailed. He probably would confront Stephanie's mom. But as she feared earlier, what if that made things worse? No matter how protective he would be, she'd still have to be at school by herself.

Her mind was a scattered mess of thoughts, making it impossible to think clearly. She just wanted to be in her room to unleash her emotions in private. The bus ride home felt endless.

# CHAPTER 22

Matthew sat in front of a plate full of deli items: salami, sliced turkey, pimento loaf, pastrami, tomato and cheese slices, and a salt and vinegar bottle. He'd fallen in love with submarine sandwiches in the last ten years. The bigger and meatier, the better.

Taking two open slices of a six-inch Italian roll, he put mayonnaise on one and mustard on the other.

He slapped the lunch meats onto the mayo roll with a "Bam" sound effect each time, smiling at the running joke he had with Sherry, Monica, and Allie in which he'd open a sandwich shop called Matty's Sandwiches.

Each teased him relentlessly. They especially made fun of his sandwich-making quirks, which he defended vigorously as he really believed that the order of the meat mattered. They'd mimic his saying, "If you change the order, you change the flavor."

Whenever he and Sherry would debate over this, she'd say she was really close to driving him to the loony bin.

He put the finishing touches on his latest sandwich creation, placing the rolls together with the right amount of pressure. Nothing should squeeze out. That was another thing they found funny.

This sandwich was one of the thicker ones he'd made, and it was perfect. "This is art," he said, marveling at his creation.

He heard the front door open and close. "Allie, you gotta see this sandwich," he yelled to her. "It should be in a museum."

She didn't answer as she beelined straight to her room. He sat a moment, again wondering if he should check on her. It wasn't like her to not greet him at all. He didn't want to overreact, and he didn't want to pry if she didn't want to offer anything. But not greeting him had to mean she was upset, and if she was hurting, he wanted to be there for her.

With a little trepidation, he headed to her room and softly knocked on her door. "Al, can I come in?"

She didn't answer at first, then quietly said, "Yeah."

He went in to see Allie sitting on her bed, her eyes red and watery. He sat next to her. She put her head on his shoulder as he put his arm around her.

She told him what had happened. So many emotions swirled: anger, upset, worry, shock. He told

Allie they needed to talk about this further, but first he wanted to call Becca's mom to check that she was okay.

Becca's mom picked up after a few rings. She told him that Becca was going to be expelled and that Stephanie's mom wanted to file a police report. And Becca wasn't really talking about it, except to say she wasn't sorry.

He told her he'd call again later after talking things over with Allie and that maybe he could help deal with the school.

As he walked back into Allie's room, he had to put his anger aside because she needed him right now. He'd deal with Stephanie's mom and the school later. He didn't know how; he just knew he would.

He sat back on Allie's bed. "I wish like anything I could protect you from things like this," he said. "But the world is..." he trailed off, trying to think of the right words when Allie interjected, "Mean."

"Mean, yeah," he said. "Sometimes it is. People can be awful. You can't control that. So you have to try your best to control you."

"How do you control your own hurt?" she asked.

"Don't know if you can," he replied. "Part of being human. One of the tougher parts."

"We used to be friends. It doesn't make sense."

"Who knows why someone develops ugliness in their heart. It's all guessing."

They sat in silence as a tear ran down Allie's face.

"You have a good heart, Allie," he consoled. "You have to keep reminding yourself that that ugliness in them has nothing to do with you. Let your own good heart lead—through the fogginess. That's what life can be sometimes. A fog."

They sat in silence for another few seconds.

"Like Rudolph," he continued. "He led through that night. Snow and fog."

That made her chuckle a little.

"I'm sticking with that," he said.

She leaned into him again, still struggling with it.

"Besides the Rudolph thing, is what I'm saying making any sense?" he asked.

"I guess," she said hesitantly.

"Will you try to control only what you can control?"

Allie gave a half-hearted shrug.

"If you want me to sleep even half-well at night, I need to hear you'll at least try," he said.

Allie replied with a muted, "I'll try."

"I need a much better 'I'll try' than that," he said. "Otherwise, I'm gonna have to do something."

Even though he said it in a jokey-type way, she asked with curiosity, "What?"

"Ohh, I got something big," he said. "You'll love it."

He could tell she was expecting one of his bursts of silliness, and seemed open to it, so he began, "First, I go to your school. Then I barge into the office, bolt the door and get right on the intercom."

Allie held in a laugh as she shook her head while he continued.

"And I say with a booming voice, 'Listen up peeps!' I'm gonna throw in peeps for coolness. 'This is Allie's daddy and he's here to tell ya'—his little girl is perfect.'"

She then gave in to a little laugh, putting her head in her hands at the mere thought.

He stood with an embellished stance and continued, "And then, wait, it gets even better. I hit the hallway and do the Ray Lewis dance the whole way down."

He started doing his best impression of Ray Lewis when he'd dance before Baltimore Raven's games to fire the home crowd up. As Matthew did it, he kept saying exaggeratedly, "This is Allie's daddy—and his little girl's perfect."

She couldn't help but laugh at his ridiculousness.

He finally finished dancing and pulled her up into a hug.

"Let me hear you say, 'You'll try' with some conviction or I'll do it," he said. "The whole hallway. I'll do it."

"I'll try," Allie said, laughing.

"Louder. I need to hear it."

"I'll try," Allie said, laughing harder.

"Good," he said, then put his hands solemnly on her shoulders. "Will you really try?"

She took a moment, getting back into a more serious mindset, then gave a little yes nod. He kissed her on the head.

"Good. Now someone's gotta get back to their sandwich. Might be my best ever."

As he was leaving, Allie said, "Did you steal the Rudolph thing from the elf dentist?"

"How dare you," he said as he left, hearing her laugh again.

His sandwich could wait, even though he was hungry. He needed to call Becca's mom back first and then start figuring out his own game plan.

Before he got too far away from Allie's door, he heard her play their song with Bob Marley belting out the lyrics, *"Everything's gonna be all right."* He allowed himself a small smile. That was his girl.

# CHAPTER 23

The more Matthew thought about Allie's school situation, the more it filled him with rage. But he also understood any rageful actions he took might make things worse for Allie.

Handling things would require a deft touch. He left a voicemail with Stephanie's mom, Cindy, that they needed to talk. It took two days before she got back to him.

"That girl should be in juvenile detention," Cindy said. "She attacked my daughter."

"I'm not going to spend a lot of time talking about Becca. Your daughter told her to kill herself. That's who you've raised."

"You know nothing about us. Stephanie and Allie haven't been friends for years."

"I know Stephanie's cruel. You have a cruel daughter. She was a bully in middle school and she's even worse now."

"How do you know Stephanie's not the one being bullied? She was the one who was punched."

"Oh, shut up. You just can't handle the fact you've raised a mean, cruel bully."

"Don't talk to me like that."

"I'm going to make things very clear. If Stephanie doesn't stop bullying Allie, things are going to get very, very ugly between you and I."

"What does that mean?"

"Let's not find out. Make it stop."

He hung up, still furious. He didn't want or expect to get that angry, but when she defended Stephanie, he couldn't help it. And he didn't know the specifics of what he'd do, but he'd make it known publicly what was going on. And he'd keep confronting Cindy, privately and publicly.

He initially got to know her when Stephanie and Allie were friends. She was a single mom; the dad not in the picture at all anymore, and she never seemed fully invested in parenting. In any circumstance she always seemed to give the bare minimum. He didn't let Allie sleep over there once he started feeling that way about her.

He wasn't maniacal in making sure Allie ate nutritiously and had a healthy environment, but he felt he did a pretty good job. When Allie stayed over at Stephanie's once, she told him all there was to eat for dinner was sugar cereal.

When Stephanie began bullying Allie in middle school, Cindy was initially apologetic and expressed how hard it was to raise Stephanie. He had some empathy for her tough situation, but she obviously did nothing about it and showed no remorse this time.

Dealing with Cindy was only half of it. He wanted to know why the school did such a poor job of policing their kids.

Heading to the meeting with Allie's principal, Karen, he recognized he was still in furious mode and reminded himself all that mattered was ensuring Allie was protected. If he lost his cool, the meeting may be counterproductive. But he was also not going to allow Stephanie to bully Allie anymore.

He sat across from Karen in her office. She appeared to be in her 40s. The office was spacious, and several certificates and framed photos of past graduating classes were on the walls. There was also a poster that said, *Dream Big, Work Hard, Stay Humble*, with an image of a girl reaching for the stars.

"How on earth is Stephanie not kicked out?" he said.

"We have a process to go through with these things. Everything needs to be evaluated."

"When a person tells another person to kill themselves, what more evaluation is needed?"

"I very much sympathize with where you're coming from, but that happened on social media after school hours. Becca's actions were during school, on school property."

"And what about all of Stephanie's bullying on the school's property? The locker room incident that the gym teacher verified."

"I agree we need to do a better job of policing that kind of behavior."

"What does that mean, specifically?"

"We're internally reviewing all of our processes. Seeing how we can better identify behaviors that lead to instances of bullying or violence."

"I'm sorry, that sounds like bureaucratic nonsense speak."

"Mr. Russell, I appreciate your anger at the situation, but there are multiple variables involved, and multiple parents involved. I assure you we will be doing all we can to keep the school the safest environment we can."

"I am angry. And if anything like this continues with my daughter, you'll see me even angrier."

He got up and left, not giving her a chance to respond. He knew she knew he was serious.

He drove home, not wanting to speak to Allie's teachers yet. Not until he calmed down. He had a good relationship with most of them and felt the conversations wouldn't be productive if he was in anger mode. What mattered most was getting a positive result out of this for Allie.

As he reached his home and turned onto his driveway, he saw Monica sitting on his front doorstep. He almost forgot to brake. That's how surprised he

was. As he looked at her, a swirl of emotions over-
came him. His anger, which was still there, was now
competing with joy. And butterflies. The good kind.
And then a rush of thoughts. Why'd she come unan-
nounced? How long would she be staying? What were
her hopes for the visit?

She looked a little nervous as she waved.

He got out of his car as she walked over to him.
"Oh my," he said. "The queen of the drop by."

"Is it okay?"

"Yeah, of course."

They shared a big hug that lingered. Finally separating, they walked into the house. He was almost at
a loss for words, but bantering with her was just so
natural; that's where his mind went.

"Did the tourists find Comoros and chase you out?"

"Thankfully, no. Just had my fill."

They went into the house, Monica sitting on the
couch in the living room as Matthew opened a glass
of Pinot Blanc.

They sat together with their wine, a little unsure at
first what to talk about.

She asked about Allie. The most natural thing to
ask about, but it jolted him back to his reality. He gave
her a recap of the bullying incident and aftermath,
and she listened attentively.

While he was telling her, he figured she didn't
come all this way to hear about his daughter's drama,
but again, it was his reality.

"That's horrible," Monica said. "Teenagers can be so cruel."

"Yeah, they can."

"How's she doing now?"

"I'm not sure I know what the definition of 'okay' is with teenagers."

"You mentioned once she had a therapist. You think that's helped?"

"Don't know," he answered. "I hope so. She's always been a sensitive kid."

"Your brother was super sensitive."

"And his partner, Kim, Allie's mom. She was even more so."

"You do your very best for her. You should be proud of that."

"Yeah. When she leaves the house, though, I'm apparently not allowed to put her in bubble wrap and just pipe in happy music. Some pesky law against it."

"I want that for me."

"I have your next birthday present, then."

They both chuckled.

"When do you leave for North Carolina?"

"Spring break's about three weeks away."

"That gives us some time together," she said with a hopeful but slightly awkward smile, as if she wasn't sure it was appropriate to pivot back to her and him.

He smiled back, reassuring her it was appropriate. "Does that mean this isn't a quick pop-in visit?"

She didn't answer right away. Finally, "I miss us," she said.

He reached for her hand. It felt so good to touch her. Their hands instantly caressed—when he got a text notification. It was Allie's English teacher. The one with which she had the best relationship.

"Fatherhood calls?" she asked.

Matthew glanced at the text and nodded. "Her teacher must have heard about my terse meeting with the principal. She'd like me to come and talk."

He looked at her as he knew the text broke the mood. But she seemed to understand.

"Would it be weird if I was here when Allie gets back?"

"No, I'll tell her you're here," he said. "She's met you enough on our chats, so she knows you a little."

"First time in person."

"She'll tease me about not giving you cooties or something."

"Do kids today know cooties?"

"Whatever today's version of cooties is, is what she'll tease me about."

They smiled.

"Try to leave some wine for me," he said, getting up.

"That's no fun," she said, also getting up.

They smiled again and looked at each other a tad awkwardly, but then both went in for a kiss. It felt good. They smiled again.

# CHAPTER 24

"Your gym teacher was the only one who wasn't super sympathetic," Matthew said to Allie as they drove away from her school. "The rest were very apologetic and promised to keep a look out."

"Can you get me out of gym?"

"I thought about that, too. I'll look into it. But Ms. Donald knows me now. I made it clear I'll go after her job if anyone messes with you."

Allie looked out the window.

"I know you're worried that this all could make things worse. But putting sunshine on something is better than keeping it in the dark."

"I don't know if I'm real worried about that anymore. Maybe a little bit. But it's embarrassing. I needed my dad to come in and solve my problems."

"I get that. But the problem needed to stop."

"Yeah. Her and her friends now just pretend I don't exist."

"Count that as a blessing. She's a lousy human."

"Yeah."

"I have some news, though. Monica came to visit. She's at the house."

Allie whip-turned towards him. "How was that not the first thing you said when you picked me up?"

He laughed. "I just met with your teachers. It felt weird not to start with that."

She rolled her eyes, which made him laugh again.

"How long is she visiting for?" Allie asked with a mix of excitement and curiosity.

"I don't know," he answered. "Would you be cool with it if she sticks around for a while?"

"Yes. I hope she does… Try not to give her cooties."

"I told her you'd say that," he said with a chuckle. "We weren't sure the youths of today knew what cooties were."

"Everyone knows cooties."

Matthew pulled into his driveway. Monica sat on the front doorstep again. She and Allie locked eyes. A shy smile and a wave from each.

# CHAPTER 25

"I've held back on some things I could tell you about him, Allie," Monica said as she ate shrimp linguini. They had gone to Matthew and Allie's favorite seafood restaurant, Oceans. He ordered his usual sea bass with some fried shrimp, and Allie went with something she never ordered before: Bouillabaisse with shrimp and clams. A very grown-up choice that he would tease her about later, as it was obvious she wanted to appear sophisticated.

"Oh, please spill," Allie pleaded.

"There's nothing to tell," Matthew said, laughing. "I've lived a normal, gossip-free life."

"A bit of a playboy, he was," Monica said.

"A playboy, huh?" Allie asked, intrigued.

"Not fair," Matthew said. "I was a single man. I had a date or two."

"Two?" Monica asked, chuckling. "Math was never his strong suit."

"You know there's so many things we could be talking about," Matthew said, smiling. "Like climate change. That's a fun topic."

Matthew was happy that Allie was having a good time. He hadn't seen her smile and laugh like this in a while.

"Can you count how many dates you've had?" Allie asked.

He laughed uncomfortably as he pawed at his sea bass.

"We've got him squirming," Monica said, clearly enjoying it.

"You're the only date I remember," Matthew said.

"What a politician," Monica guffawed.

"I like this squirming thing, Dad," Allie said. "I could get used to it."

"I have two words for that. Ki and bosh," Matthew said.

"Almost positive kibosh is one word," Allie replied.

"She's a smart one," Monica said. "And it's still weird for me to hear you called 'dad.'"

"Ha! I'd actually say 'dad' defines me more than anything else." Then he turned to Allie. "My little pumpkin over here," he said teasingly.

Allie put her head in her hands and said, "Oh God."

"Squirming can go both ways," Matthew said. "And I needed the title to tell my dad jokes."

"They're really, really bad," Allie said. "Should be outlawed."

"Never. They're all gold. Each one funnier than the last."

"Dreamer," Allie retorted. "And then those awful sandwiches you make. Banished."

"Brilliant sandwiches. If not so tasty, they should reside in museums."

"They don't even fit in your mouth. You have to practically break your jaw each time you eat one."

"You're grounded. One whole year."

"As long as I don't have to eat one of the sandwiches."

Matthew noticed that his and Allie's bantering had left Monica out of the conversation. She didn't appear bothered by it, but he changed the subject to her travels. He knew Allie would love to hear about any adventure she hadn't already shared, and she had many.

Monica regaled them with one particular story about living in Bolivia for six months.

"The Aymara New Year happens on June 21st and is a national holiday for them. The celebration is wild."

"Is it like our New Year's celebration in Times Square?" Allie asked.

"Some cities may be similar, but I was lucky enough to spend it at the Inca site of Tiwanaku. Thousands gathered to watch as the sun rose over these incredible-looking ancient megalithic structures. Some of them were built back in 200 BC."

Matthew and Allie both said, "Wow."

"It also marks the winter solstice in the Southern Hemisphere so they're celebrating that, too."

Matthew could tell Monica's storytelling transfixed Allie, her curiosity itch getting the greatest scratch.

He also enjoyed it and sat back, enjoying the three of them together this way. But he also couldn't help thinking that the mundane life he led in a suburb of Phoenix was no comparison to anything Monica had experienced. It reminded him of Kenny's dilemma. Playing football was in his DNA, just like world hopping was in hers. Could she actually go from something really exciting to a life that was not even close to being exciting?

He hoped so. With her here now, they'd certainly be finding out.

# CHAPTER 26

"Is her being here throwing you for a loop at all?" Sherry asked Allie as they drank hot chocolate in Sherry's kitchen after her father dropped her off from the restaurant.

"I mean it was a whoa moment, but a good one."

"Those two have been driving me crazy since college. On then off over and over. Put a real crimp in my 'settin' people up' rep."

Allie laughed. "That's so inconsiderate of them."

"I couldn't agree more," Sherry said, chuckling. "But now, you know your daddy. 'Mr. Worries Too Much.' Will he give it a chance if she does?"

"Do you think she was the love of his life?"

"Yes."

"But that was a while back."

"It was. Love doesn't always make sense. For some, it goes away. For others, it doesn't. With them, who knows? I don't think they even know."

"I'm afraid I'd be the reason it doesn't work."

"No, no, no. Don't do that to yourself."

"I mean his first decision was saying it'd just be me and him going to North Carolina."

"Of course it's just you and him. You're going there to learn about your mama. She understands that; if she doesn't, that's on her."

"But don't you think he's always going to prioritize me? How's that supposed to make her feel?"

"Sweetie, you've gotta get out of your head on this. Their relationship is all on them. If they want it bad enough, they'll find a way."

Allie sighed and chuckled. "I think 'Mr. Worries Too Much' has a daughter who's inherited that gene."

"That's what I'm here for. To beat it out of ya'. Or at least tickle it out of 'ya." Sherry tickled her and Allie laughed.

But like father like daughter, Allie was similar when it came to worrying. She couldn't help it. She worried about his future. If he wouldn't make a relationship work, whether because of her or not, what would happen when she was an adult and had a life of her own? What if Monica wouldn't ever give him another chance? Would his fatherly devotion leave him a lonely person? She wished she could stop worrying about that, but how could she? Despite what he always said, she was a reason he was still single. Maybe the main reason.

Nothing would make her happier than her dad being happy. And she didn't think he was unhappy at all, but maybe Monica could bring a different kind of happiness. It was obvious he lit up when he was around her. And they bantered well. Allie figured that's why they probably hit it off so well from the beginning. Her dad loved to banter.

She also liked Monica. And was fascinated by her. She had such incredible adventures and was a great storyteller. She'd been to almost everywhere on earth and could speak about each location as if she were part of that place's tourist board. It all sounded so appealing. She looked forward to getting to know her even more.

And she'd also try giving them any space they needed. Her school issues made for horrible timing, though. She and her dad were going to have another talk about whether she should be homeschooled. If she was, he'd have to be more hands-on. And that was yet another thing that might make things with Monica tougher. But without Becca at school, could she really handle it? Should she force herself to join a club there in the hopes she'd like it?

She knew people in all the clubs and didn't like the idea of spending time with them. But was it fair to her father if she didn't try?

She didn't want to give herself a headache thinking about it, but she had to make a choice. And unfortunately, it did give her a headache.

# CHAPTER 27

"I'm so used to paying now since it's just Allie and me," Matthew said. "Sorry about that."

"Not a big deal," Monica replied. "We always went Dutch, so I wasn't expecting it."

Matthew had dropped Allie at Sherry's, and he and Monica went to Tempe Beach Park. Sitting on a bench overlooking the glistening water, they held hands and talked.

"To make up for my faux pas, I'll let you buy me a car."

"How about your old Audi? I'll find it and offer any price."

"Now we're talking," Matthew said, chuckling.

She chuckled back and leaned into him as they looked at the water.

"Just things I need to get used to," Monica said. "How close you two are. How much her life occupies yours."

"It ebbs and flows. You picked an ... ebbing time."

"Timing's never been one of our allies."

"I haven't had to get used to balancing too much in a while. Like right before I saw you at my house, I was the angriest I'd been in a long time. And then I kind of shelved that while also not completely shelving it. It was a very odd feeling."

"Were you happy to see me?"

"I think you know the answer to that," he said with a smile.

She smiled back. "Hopefully Allie was okay with it, too."

"She was. She's always wanted to meet you in person. I just hope we didn't make you feel too third-wheelish."

"No, it was fun. She even banters like you."

"I told her she'd have to pay rent if she didn't learn how to banter."

"Your parenting strategies are remarkable. You should write a book."

He laughed. "I wish she could banter with others, though. It's me, her friend Becca, Sherry and maybe Kenny. With everyone else, she's deadly quiet."

"That's common for introverts. They have to be comfortable. Not like extroverted you."

"Do you think I'm an extrovert? I think I'm neither."

"Yeah, I guess you're not. I'm the same. It's always situational."

"My old GPS device would say when I took a new route, 'recalibrating,'" he said. "I think that's kinda' what we're going to do a little."

"A little recalibrating probably never hurt anyone."

They smiled and just looked at each other, appreciating the moment together. She went and sat on his lap, and they started kissing. Finally, she put her head on his shoulder.

"I want to try this time," she said.

He smiled. More kissing.

"I'm sure you're wondering what's changed about me."

"I was just thinking how I'd phrase that question."

"I don't know if I'd call it changed." She took a moment to gather her thoughts. "I feel full. From the life I've led."

"That lifestyle has been your everything."

"It has. But I've done it for a while. And I don't know if I'm missing … another kind of life."

"I guess you can't know unless you experience another type of life."

"No, you can't."

They sat in silence.

She finally spoke. "If things had happened differently, would you have … come to Spain?"

He paused before saying, "I don't know."

She put her head back on his shoulder and he rubbed her neck. The uncertainty about what the future held for them didn't matter at that moment. This felt so right. And he wanted to just bathe in it. But making things work might be like walking a tightrope. There was a reason it'd never worked previously. Mostly because neither wanted to compromise. And compromise wasn't on the table anymore for him, as his decisions were no longer just his own. Allie not getting hurt by however their relationship shook out was a major priority.

He and Allie briefly talked before they went to dinner with Monica. She reminded him of something he'd told her often, "Life's a ride and the destination, for the most part, is unknown. So try your best to enjoy the ride." He told her how he'd worry she'd get hurt, and she said she'd be more hurt if he didn't try, especially because of her. So, he was going take their advice—and go on this ride.

# CHAPTER 28

I t would have been too difficult for Allie to eat lunch in the cafeteria without Becca, so she ate by herself under a tree in the schoolyard. She had begun packing her own lunch, this time a salami sandwich, an apple and a Mars bar.

While still on school property, she was far enough away from the groups of students eating together at picnic tables. This is where she missed Becca the most.

As she ate, a squirrel came nearby. Animals coming near freaked her out when she was younger, but taking so many photos in nature made her feel comfortable with them now. She still hated insects, though.

"Hello there," she said to the squirrel, pulling her camera out of her backpack. The squirrel sniffed around for food and she took photos.

"You're no Becca, but I'm going to let you be my friend... No, no, don't get emotional. I'm a regular person, just like you... And I know it's special, seeing as how I have only one other friend. But you and me, we're good."

A car screeched in the parking lot—and the squirrel ran off.

"Until next time!" Allie yelled after.

She got a text from Becca: *How's it going?*

*I'm talking to squirrels*, Allie texted back.

*So, normal*, Becca wrote, followed by three 'laughing hard with tears' emojis. *Yep*, Allie wrote, adding the same three emojis. Then,

*How r u?*

*Okay. Haven't met any Stephanie types, so that's a win.*

*Big win.*

*Hope gym doesn't suck for ya'.*

*If she and her friends keep pretending I don't exist, should be fine.*

The bell rang.

*Bell. Gotta go.*

*Talk later.*

They texted at lunch every day and still saw each other frequently after school, although in shorter increments because Becca's new school was forty-five minutes away and she got home later.

Allie headed towards the school entrance when she suddenly saw a guy walking toward her, about a hundred yards away. Her heart started pounding. There was nothing for her to do but keep walking. She didn't know him, but he looked like he was a junior or senior, with a wisp of a mustache and close to six feet. What did he want? Breathing became harder, and her heart pounded fast. She didn't want to cry but felt it bubbling up. *Don't cry*, she urged herself silently as he got closer, but still not close enough to speak.

Her heart now felt like a million miles an hour when he got about fifteen feet away. He was going to speak.

"You took that photo of the school where you gave it kind of a gothic look, right?"

It took her a moment to catch her breath, but then she nodded quickly and said, "Uh huh," way too fast.

"I really liked it," he said. "I'm on the yearbook committee. Can we use it?"

"Uhh, okay," she said, with a bit of a stunned look.

"Cool. Thanks," he said, then turned around and headed back to the school entrance. She followed but slowed down so she wouldn't be too close. Her heart was slowing, and she still wanted to cry. Going from fear to getting complimented was overwhelming. She didn't know how to react. But she took a few deep breaths and held any tears at bay. Then she laughed and thought, *What was her life?*

# CHAPTER 29

Allie sat on her bed looking at her suitcase in the corner of the room when her dad stuck his head in.

"Did you ever look up all the YouTube packing hacks?" he asked.

"Yeah."

"And? Is it going to change every way I've thought about packing?"

"There's good stuff," she said. "They all made sense."

"Well, that's all I need then." He started to leave.

"Dad," she said, then paused. He turned back. "I don't think I want to go."

He looked surprised at first but then came over and sat next to her. Spring Break was a few days away. Their North Carolina trip was fully planned. Besides trying to meet as many people as possible who knew her mother, they were also going to visit several rivers throughout the state, as her father arranged with his magazine to shoot a rivers theme, an idea he wanted to do in as many states as possible. And she loved the idea of taking her own river shots as well. But the timing of going there just felt wrong. Monica had been here a few weeks, and it was going well.

"Are you doing this for me, Al?" he asked.

"Going now doesn't feel right. You guys are in the middle of figuring things out. That's more important."

"You're more important. Learning about your mom is something you've wanted for a long time. Monica and I can handle being away for two weeks."

"But I really don't want to go. I can learn about her some other time."

He looked at her as if trying to gauge what was in her head. Then he sighed. "Well, we got ourselves a little conundrum, don't we?"

"I know you paid for the tickets and everything. I'm sorry."

"And my boss was really excited about the rivers theme."

"Oh... I didn't think about that."

"It's secondary. Doing what's best for you comes first."

"I know you didn't think Monica should come with us. But that was when she first got here."

"That hasn't changed. She and I both agreed that didn't feel right."

"Did she agree?"

He chuckled. "It's a complicated thing. It didn't feel right to me. And she ultimately understood that."

"I'll go if you need to for work."

"No. I believe you when you say you don't want to go. I've built up enough goodwill with Phil. He won't love it, but he'll understand."

"Thank you," she said, hugging him.

"We were going to have a lot of time to talk in North Carolina. Especially about whether to homeschool you."

"I've been thinking about that, too. I'm not ready for it."

He looked surprised.

"I may change my mind. But I like most of my teachers. And since the incident, some people have been nicer. Plus, I don't want to feel like someone's making me run away."

He smiled and hugged her. "I'm proud of you."

"I did say I might change my mind."

"I'll still be proud of 'ya."

"Just as much?"

He laughed. "Maybe an inch less. Or a millimeter."

She smiled. "I'll take it."

Her father left, and she put her suitcase back in the closet then lay on the bed. The school choice was tough as she was on the fence over it. For some reason, she wanted to stick it out for as long as she could. Knowing there was a homeschool option helped. And it was possible she could make more friends. She'd just take it day by day.

And she was really happy they weren't going to North Carolina anymore. She liked Monica and her father together. It made her feel good on many levels. He was happy. She was awesome to be around. Their relationship had momentum, if that was a thing. She didn't know if it was, but it made sense.

And so the thought of possibly breaking that momentum made her upset. What if being apart for two weeks put a damper on things to the point where one of them changed their mind? While she didn't think that was likely, she didn't want to find out either.

# CHAPTER 30

The next few weeks were amazing for Matthew. He and Monica did all the couples type things they could think of.

Gondola ride. Check. Champagne picnic under a tree. Check. However, that one came with a mishap in that he wasn't a champagne guy and hadn't opened a bottle in a while. As he uncorked it, all the while giving her a sexy gaze, the champagne exploded out. They both jumped out of the way just in time and had a good laugh about it.

He wasn't sure whether the romantic aspect would feel the same as it once did. But it didn't take very long to realize that it did. And he loved it even more than he thought he would.

And he was glad Allie chose not to go to North Carolina. He didn't want to leave Monica at that moment. Part of that, he realized, stemmed from the fact she could change her mind about their relationship while he was gone. It was irrational, but they had never been able to make it work before, so it was hard for him to feel completely on solid ground with her.

As for Allie, he didn't really worry that she felt any upset about all the time he was spending with Monica—but she quashed any thought of it when she told him one morning, "I'm nipping in the bud any kind of thoughts you might have that you're neglecting me somehow." He chuckled and gave her a hug.

Monica scheduled a spa day, which allowed Matthew and Sherry to get in a game of darts. Since they hadn't been doing their competitions lately, the trash-talking intensified. He won slightly and she wanted a rematch soon. Neither knew when, but they both agreed that no matter what was going on in their lives, they had to find time for their competitions.

\* \* \*

"Talk to me," Matthew said to Allie as he and she stood on a big rock at the edge of Lake Patagonia. She was taking photos of the tranquil blue water and the uneven peaks of the Patagonia Mountains that surrounded them.

"I'm trying to get the angle to catch the light as it bounces," Allie replied.

"What made you start with that angle?"

"Wouldn't you have started with it?" Allie asked, looking over at him.

"Not necessarily," he said. "You chose it because it felt right. Always trust your instincts like that."

Allie nodded okay and started taking photos again.

With North Carolina out and spring break now here, Matthew had suggested a day trip. Allie and Monica were down for it. He loved how they had bonded.

Monica sat on a bench nearby, watching them. The air was crisp and clean, and besides some bird calls, the only sounds were the gentle lapping of the water against the shore. In the distance they could see some kayakers moving across the lake.

Allie had suggested Lake Patagonia, as she wanted to photograph certain things there. An excursion with both of them was bliss. Everything about it gave him joy. They had blasted music and sang most of the three-hour ride. Monica and Allie agreed that if he sang less, it would be better, not just for them, but for the world in general. He returned their insult by singing louder, which made them laugh. It was a fun drive.

Monica had been a little surprised at Allie's decision to forego North Carolina, but he could tell she was also relieved.

He allowed himself to think that one day the three of them might take vacations together. But then he reminded himself not to get too far ahead of things.

He looked over at Monica sitting on the bench. She was looking down at her phone, seemingly absorbed by something. He wondered if she was bored, but she eventually looked over at them and smiled.

Allie put her camera down and looked around, seeing another area of interest on the lake. "Look where the currents intersect and the shadows," she remarked to Matthew. "Can we get me closer? That'll be amazing."

He looked at the area she was referring to and said, "If I hold you off the ledge and you can really lean in."

"Let's do it," Allie said enthusiastically.

They walked to the ledge, and he grabbed the back of her shirt as she leaned in.

"Don't tilt too far; you may pull both of us in," Matthew said.

"This shot would be worth it," Allie replied.

"Speak for yourself. We've got a long drive home."

"A little further," Allie said, straining to reach where she wanted.

Matthew let her go a little further, struggling to hold her.

"Is that safe?" Monica asked.

"I'm good," Allie said. "Further, Dad."

"I can't go much further."

He let her go a tiny bit further, and Allie started taking pictures. "I'm getting it," she said giddily.

Matthew still struggled and started slipping a little.

"Whoa, whoa," Monica said.

Allie and Matthew almost fell in—but he pulled back with all his strength to reel Allie in and back to the ledge. Allie laughed.

"At least one of us found it funny," Matthew said.

"The shot is amazing," Allie replied. "Look." She showed him the shot, and she was right. It was gorgeous and creative.

"Wow," he said. "I guess it was worth it. Let's not do it again, though."

He jokingly nudged her as if to knock her into the water. She laughed and did it back to him.

Matthew smiled and looked over at Monica, who was back looking at her phone.

"Try not to fall in," Matthew said to Allie as he walked over to Monica and sat with her. She gave him a smile.

"You're not bored, are you?" he asked.

"No. It's beautiful here."

"Something on your phone's got your attention."

She took a second, then said, "Just some work stuff I'm looking into. Got to make decisions about that."

He nodded okay. He was still adjusting to her being here. The great times when they'd go on picnics and hikes and have meaningful talks were mixed with moments of uncertainty. He sometimes sensed that the routine nature of his life made her bored. She'd say she wasn't, but it didn't always feel sincere.

"You came here as a kid, right?"

"Yeah, it's where my mom first introduced me to real photography."

"Nostalgic then, huh?"

"I fed off her passion for it."

"And Allie's fed off your passion for it."

"The circle of life," he said, smiling.

"Too bad I didn't know you then. The embarrassing things about you that I share with her only goes back so far."

"I'm hoping you'll run out of embarrassing stories soon."

"I'm about halfway there," she said as she poked him in the ribs playfully.

"Sherry and Kenny ran out of them years ago, so I thought I was out of the woods," he said, smiling.

"Happy to give Allie new ammunition," she said.

He was about to head back to Allie to see what photos she was capturing when he saw an email notification from a law firm. As he opened it, he was instantly shocked. Cindy had gotten a restraining order against him. It made him laugh.

"What?" Monica said.

Matthew showed her the email. "Wow," she said. "The bully's mom thinks you bullied her."

"Looks that way. Pretty pathetic."

They left shortly thereafter, as he didn't want to get home too late. The ride home was more somber with the Cindy situation now on his mind. It was annoying and he preferred just to ignore it as he didn't want to interact with her in any way. But if Stephanie started bullying Allie again, he needed to know what recourse he'd have, as his terse conversation with Cindy seemed to have made a difference.

He peeked over at Monica, who stared out the window, respecting his somber mood. He wondered what she was thinking. She had led a mostly stress-free life by herself. His life would probably never be stress-free. That had to bother her on some level. When she envisioned coupling up with him, did she only ever think about the good times they'd have? Was she prepared for his stuff to become her stuff? Probably not. But if she wanted to be with him badly enough, she'd accept it. That would be the question that always gnawed at him—how bad did she want to be with him? When they were young, she chose her dream of world-hopping. What was her dream now?

He looked at Allie in the rearview mirror to see her sleeping. He really wanted Monica to stay and for them to create a life together. But if she ultimately decided against it, he would understand. His life was what it was. And it wouldn't be changing.

# CHAPTER 31

"She's fearless when she's taking pics," Monica said as she and Matthew sat on his couch.

He laughed as he drank a Corona. Monica was trying to take his mind off the Cindy situation.

"What?" she asked, swishing her glass of Merlot, before sipping.

"Never thought that word would be used with her," he said. "And I'm tempted to wake her so she can hear it."

"But she was."

"Yeah," he said. "Proud of her... I mean, she still has her anxiety. Think she'll always be somewhat like that. But in other ways she won't be. And I love that for her."

It'd been a strange day. When they got home from the lake, he was served with a form labeled SV-110, which meant a judge had granted a temporary restraining order against him. He talked with a lawyer and learned that if he didn't follow all the orders granted by the judge, he could be arrested and charged with a crime. And on another form, SV-109, he was given a court date two weeks away whereupon the judge would decide whether to grant the restraining order against him, one that could last up to three years. He would, however, have the option to tell the judge that he didn't agree with it. He already was ruminating about how he'd detail all of Stephanie's bullying—and Cindy's negligence in dealing with it.

He could tell Monica was made very uncomfortable by it all. They didn't need to discuss it to know his time would now be dominated by dealing with it, at least until it was resolved.

Monica swished her glass again as if she was unsure how to converse with him in the moment. "Sherry thinks we're not actually talking," she said.

"She still calls you 'Wanderlust.'"

"Do you think we're actually talking?"

He took a few seconds. "Yes... And probably no. We skate over some things."

Monica gave a small nod. They sat in more silence. Finally, she said, "Your connection with her. It's still hard for me to get used to."

"Really?"

"Yeah, it's not just how I didn't see that for you when we first met... It's ... your connection is strong. Unique."

He let out an "Mmm" with a little look of suspicion.

"What?" she asked.

"Kinda' feels like you might be leading somewhere with this."

"No." She paused. "Your life is a … whole deal."

"Can I ask what was on your phone that had you so absorbed at the lake?"

Monica let out a nervous little laugh, then paused. Then she showed him on her phone an invite that read: *Is Kashmir calling your name? Super exclusive for members. Book now!*

He gave a knowing smile and asked, "How long?"

"Two months."

He read more of her invite, then looked at her and said, "Knew we'd hit this fork at some point."

"I told you we wouldn't."

They looked at each other. Small smiles as not having words yet. She reached for his hand, and they clasped fingers tenderly.

"Maybe the timing is good," he said. "I'm going to be dealing with this Cindy nonsense for a bit."

She looked down and swished her glass again. "I've realized watching you." She paused as if searching for words. "Even when she's old enough to be on her own—you'll never have…" She stopped, again searching for the right words.

"Wanderlust," he said.

She nodded as she teared up. He realized this was more than just a general life conversation. "Kashmir won't be a temporary detour, will it?"

She slightly shook her head no, then stroked his hair and said, "You're the only one I've ever been drawn to."

He looked at her with a slight smile. She took his hand again and said, "It's me. Even when I sometimes wish it wasn't."

"No. It's us... You're you... And I'm me."

"I told you I had my fill of living that kind of life. I really thought I did. At my last stop in Thailand, I just started feeling so empty. Traveling and moving from place to place always filled the empty. The only other thing that ever filled the empty was you."

"What if the empty feeling comes back?"

"I don't know. What if it comes and goes? Could you handle me jumping back in and out of your life like that?"

He was trying to process everything in the moment, which was difficult. He loved her. But he also knew he couldn't handle a yo-yo existence.

"I don't think I could."

She nodded, understanding. Then, she wiped a tear and said, "Two ships," while crossing her hands over each other to signify going in different directions.

He nodded in agreement. "Two good ships."

They sat silently, being with their thoughts. Another breakup for them. Their love just never being able to overcome their differences. Like two perfectly fitting puzzle pieces, but in different boxes. It saddened him even more because this time felt final.

She was right; even when Allie was on her own, he'd never want to live her desired life—and she'd never want to live his.

He wondered if they'd keep up their video chat friendship. Neither asked about it. Right now, he thought it was best they didn't. They'd each be constantly reminded of the heartbreak. Maybe at some point they would again, but probably not in the same way.

With one final hug, Monica left. Matthew sat back on the couch and finished his Corona. The hurt was raw now, but he thought of Allie. Merely thinking of her instantly made the hurt lessen. He got to be that wonderful girl's father. Adopting her was the best, most amazing thing he'd ever done in his life. He'd do it again every time. The empty feeling Monica said she experienced—he realized he had those moments before Allie. But never since. Not even close.

# CHAPTER 32

"But you really like her," Allie said. Her father sat on her bed and just told her he and Monica had broken up. She didn't see it coming. It saddened her.

"I do," he said.

"And she likes you."

"Life—"

"Doesn't always make sense," she said, cutting him off.

He chuckled. "Have I said that once or twice?"

She looked at him, still sad. Then lay down. He looked at her, not really having words. Finally, he asked, "Do I gotta play our song? Bob Marley always gets us right."

She shook her head no. Then she sat up and gave him a hug. They stayed together for several moments.

"The thing you've said to me more than anything is 'my happiness is your happiness,'" she said. "Well, your happiness is my happiness."

Touched, he pulled her in tighter. "I'm going to be all right," he said. "Okay?"

She nodded. Life was so abrupt. Monica hadn't been in town long, but she had gotten used to the idea of her sticking around. Monica and her father seemed so great together.

But now she was gone. And she was certain her father was hurting, more than he let on. And her fear of his one day being lonely came back. That would be so unfair. He didn't deserve loneliness.

"Can I sign you up for OK Cupid?" she asked jokingly, but she also wasn't joking.

"No," he said, amused.

"Hinge?"

"No."

"E-Harmony?"

"I'm frightened you know this many. And no."

"There's a bunch more."

He laughed, kissed her head and said, "All no."

She sighed. She'd never have any control over that part of his life. But she knew she'd always be there for him. No matter what.

She suddenly felt a little bit of anger toward Monica. She didn't need to come back into his life, but she also knew she didn't hurt him on purpose. As her dad said, life didn't always make sense.

If Monica had stayed longer, she'd have been more hurt for herself. But it just felt like an extended visit. The toughest part was that they really hit it off.

"Should I stay in touch with her?"

"If you want. I think she'd like that. She really liked you."

"Okay. Can I tell her that her timing sucks because now it's too late for North Carolina?"

He chuckled. "Timing has never been her and my friend. How about we go over the summer?"

Allie nodded. "Yeah, I'll be ready then."

"Good. You okay or do you want to talk more about this?"

"I'm okay."

He kissed her on the head and left. Allie laid down. If her father couldn't make it work with someone who seemed nearly perfect for him, then how could she have optimism for any relationships? Although Sherry and Kenny had been married forever. But even with them, she sensed they were going through a rough patch. She'd never ask Sherry about it, though. And she was pretty sure Sherry would never want to talk about that with her. Even though they were close, she was more mama bear and always kept conversations about her.

With her father's situation, the ol' guilt meter always reared its head in these moments. No matter what anyone said, if she wasn't in the picture, her dad and Monica very possibly could have made things work. But at this moment, she didn't want to wallow in guilt. Instead, she wanted to be grateful for her father. He always chose her. In any instance where he could have put his own happiness first, he didn't. He was the greatest gift of her life. And that would always make her heart smile.

Tomorrow, she'd get back to feeling guilty. That thought made her chuckle, but she also knew it was probably true.

# CHAPTER 33

"Therapy ice cream sundaes may be your best idea ever," Sherry said as she and Matthew ate sundaes at their favorite ice cream shop *Cream of the Crop*. The shop was half full, which for a Tuesday afternoon was impressive. He always liked how colorful the décor was, like a rainbow exploded onto the walls.

"How is this not a thing already?" Matthew asked.

"It probably is a thing. Just maybe no one named it."

"I'll get my trademark people on it pronto."

"You do that."

They ate as a silence came over them. Frivolity aside, they were there to talk about some of the tougher things going on. They hadn't had a good life talk in a little while, but they needed one with all that was going on with both. This was more for Sherry, though, as Matthew's recent restraining order got resolved, and Sherry knew all about it already.

Matthew had attended his court date and read his statement to the judge, "Since the bullying situation came to my attention, and I spoke with the parent of the bully, the bullying has stopped. If this continues then I will happily keep my distance from the parent of the bully."

The judge then granted Cindy's restraining order for three years, which he expected. In the courtroom, Cindy wouldn't make eye contact and seemed afraid of him. He wanted her to be.

He was certain she understood that Allie wasn't to be bullied anymore. That's all he cared about.

And since he never crossed paths with Cindy anyway, it wasn't a big deal to him. The only possible nuisance was he wasn't allowed at the school if Cindy was there, but she was rarely there, so he didn't feel as if it would be a problem.

Sherry was having a tough time, though, and he wanted her to know he was there for her.

Things with Kenny were not great, and the last time they spoke she hadn't wanted to elaborate besides saying things weren't great. Amidst this rough patch, she was in a car accident while driving with Darius to pick up his brothers from their different football and basketball practices. Her car got banged up as another car made an improper turn in an intersection and clipped the back of her car, which spun and slammed into a curb. No one was hurt, but Sherry was pretty upset about it, partly because Kenny was supposed to pick up the other kids. But he overslept and didn't answer his phone.

"We gotta get to your serious stuff at some point," Matthew said.

"Why ruin things?"

"You need to tell me what's going on with Kenny."

She didn't answer right away. Finally, "It's more than his depression and lack of communication," she said heavily. "Something's happening."

He gave her a moment to give more. She didn't, instead picking at her ice cream as if she was struggling with her thoughts.

He knew from previous conversations Kenny had been spiraling, drinking more and sleeping a lot.

"C'mon, Sher. Talk to me." He wasn't used to her being this vulnerable.

"Intuition," she said after another lengthy pause. "When you've been with someone a long time."

The words made Matthew pause. She didn't elaborate, but the look she gave confirmed that she suspected Kenny might have been unfaithful. He slumped in his chair as if he had been punched in the stomach.

Sherry teared up, finally putting her head in her hands as she silently started crying.

He got up and guided her to stand, giving her a big hug. Other customers looked at them, but he didn't care. His friend needed a hug.

She slowed her crying, and gathered herself a little, asking, "Is everyone staring?"

Most had stopped looking at them, but he jokingly said, "Yes, which only helps when I trademark 'Therapy Ice Cream Sundaes.'"

She separated and laughed, wiping her eyes.

"I should get half," she joked back. "I brought the show to it."

"Deal," he said.

They didn't continue talking about Kenny. Enough was said. Sherry spoke instead about one of Darius' recent basketball games where he hit the game-winning shot at the buzzer. Talking about her kids always filled her with joy.

With their ice cream done, they both needed to get back to work. As Matthew drove home, he couldn't stop thinking about Kenny. If it was anyone else who was hurting Sherry, it would have been easy to just villainize the guy. But even with their friendship nothing like it used to be, he still considered Kenny family.

He couldn't stand the thought of him possibly cheating on Sherry, though. It made him angry. And he knew he'd have to confront him over whether it was true. It was going to be a tough conversation.

# CHAPTER 34

Matthew walked into the Foxhole, a dive bar in Phoenix that he knew Kenny frequented. It was the kind of place where they kept the lights low and the liquor flowing. A neon beer sign sat on the wooden wall behind the bar. A pool table sat in the back, and a jukebox played a rock ballad from what he thought was Foreigner.

The crowd was sparse as it was only a little after 8:00 pm. Kenny was there, sitting at the bar by himself, nursing a beer. Matthew sat on the stool next to him, which wobbled slightly. He figured most of the stools here wobbled.

Kenny looked at him, surprised. "Why do I have a feeling this ain't a 'hang out with your buddy' get-together?"

Matthew gave a slight chuckle as they sat quietly for a moment.

A bartender came over and Matthew asked for the same beer as Kenny. When the bartender filled his glass, he could see it was a Heineken.

"I can't explain me any better to you than I try to her," Kenny said.

"Who can explain who they are?"

"It's hard enough without feeling like I'm letting her down."

Matthew took a few swigs of his Heineken, took a deep breath, then asked, "Are you being unfaithful?"

Kenny didn't look at him. They sat in silence. Finally, Kenny said, "I love that woman with all my heart."

"I believe that. But?" He let the question linger in the air.

"I never … cheated," Kenny said.

"Then what is going on?"

Kenny took another long moment before finally saying, "Talking with someone who doesn't know you. They don't make you feel bad."

"You meet up with another woman to just talk?"

"Do you believe I'd cheat on her?"

"I don't want to believe it. The guy I've always known wouldn't."

"I'm still him."

Matthew stared at him. Kenny took a second but then looked back at Matthew. "I'm still him, Matty."

Matthew looked down at his beer. Then, he took a few sips. "Aren't shrinks for talking?"

Kenny didn't answer.

"Are they for people who aren't tough?" Matthew asked.

"I ain't got a problem with them."

"What do you call it if you won't go to one?"

That made Kenny laugh a little.

"She thinks you're cheating on her. And it's breaking her heart."

Kenny exhaled and rubbed his temples. His eyes became misty. "I'll talk with her."

"She needs you, man."

Kenny nodded a little, knowing it.

"Out of everyone in our friend group, she's the best of us," Matthew said. "We'd probably all be bigger messes without her."

Kenny acknowledged it with another little chuckle.

"I married a gem," Kenny said.

"Yes, you did."

They sat for a long silence. Matthew didn't know if Kenny was cheating or not. He seemed sincere in his denial. But would he actually admit it? He did believe he loved Sherry, though. And he hoped they could find a way back to the way they were.

Kenny finally turned to him. "I'm not saying you got money issues anymore, although I don't know 'cause we don't chop it up like we used to—but if you did, who'd you come to, me or Sherry?"

"One, I'm fine," Matthew said. "But two, what is this thing where it's you or her? You're both like family."

Kenny turned back forward while saying, "You didn't answer."

Matthew wasn't going to since they both knew the answer.

They sat in more silence, Matthew racking his brain for something to say to try and heal things.

But Kenny finally spoke up again. "Do you miss at all the way it was?" he asked. "After my games, you, me and the boys livin' it up."

"I don't know about the 'livin' it up' part. I miss the times we had. The camaraderie. But times change."

Kenny shook his head a little as if reminiscing. "I was good, man... I was damn good."

"You were," Matthew concurred.

They sat in more silence.

"No matter what's going on, you being right is important to me," Matthew said.

"I know how I've been. I ain't proud of it."

More silence. Kenny resumed, "You're a good dad, man. A little clingy, but you're better than I ever thought you could be."

Matthew laughed a little. "I do my best."

They sipped their beers again. "I didn't think enough about the future when I played."

"I remember talking about it a little with you back then. You figured you'd stay part of the game in some way."

"That was just something I'd say. 'Cause what else but something with ball would I be doing? But I knew I didn't have the patience to coach. And I knew calling games or talking in a studio wouldn't work, even though I know what I'd be talking about. I'd just be too mad that I wasn't playing. I can't even watch games anymore 'cause of that."

"Have you talked to any of the guys that do TV, to see how they deal with that?"

"Yeah, they said they miss playing but also love talking ball. I don't. Talking doesn't scratch the itch. I need that competitive juice. And it ain't nowhere else."

"It's been almost fifteen years since you hung it up."

"Yeah. But I feel the same way whenever I try something new. Empty."

They sat in more silence. Matthew wished he could help but didn't know how. He was glad they were communicating, though. That was probably the best route for Kenny. Keep communicating.

"I don't know the answers, but I wish you'd talk to someone. They may be as good at what they do as you were at ball."

Kenny laughed a little at that. "Except they get to keep doing it after forty."

More silence. This one lasted longer as they just drank. Finally, Matthew said, "I know when I say I'm here for you, it's just words. But I am here for you. I want you to be right."

Kenny didn't say anything for a few moments. Then he took another sip of his beer and held out his fist for Matthew to dap, which he did.

They drank together for another half hour, Matthew filling him in on Allie's recent turmoil and his brief reunion with Monica, which Kenny only knew tidbits about. He offered to help intimidate someone on Allie's behalf if needed. Matthew laughed and said, "We don't need both of us in trouble with the law."

When Matthew was ready to go, they hugged it out and agreed to find time to hang. No specifics on doing what, but it was a start.

# CHAPTER 35

*I'm actually thinking of joining the yearbook committee,* Allie texted to Becca as she sat back under her tree at lunch.

*Really??? There's some annoying ones in there,* Becca texted back.

*I know. I'll wear earplugs and just take photos,* Allie texted with a laughing face emoji.

*My little one getting brave!* Becca texted with the same laughing face emoji.

The bell went off and Allie texted, *Bell, gotta go,* and she headed back to school. She walked slowly, as she'd timed her pace so she could arrive in class just before she'd be late. But more importantly, it meant avoiding a crowded hallway.

As she got inside, she saw a commotion down the hallway. The guy on the yearbook committee who complimented her a little while back had a smaller kid pinned against a locker. Neither of them saw her as she froze.

"You think it was funny saying I had a big ego in front of my girl?" the guy yelled at the other kid.

The smaller kid replied, "It was just a joke. I'm sorry."

The guy slammed the kid's face into the locker. "Next time, it'll be worse," he yelled before storming off the other way, never seeing Allie.

She saw that the right side of the kid's face was reddened by the locker impact, and he had tears in his eyes.

Then he saw Allie, still standing frozen.

"Are you okay?" she said, but he ran off the other way before she finished the sentence. Allie sighed, shook her head and walked to class. She just didn't understand why humans were so awful to each other—and that there were so often no consequences for it.

She actually knew the smaller kid a little. He was in her math class. She thought his name was Eric. He was kind of obnoxious and liked making fart noises in class, which would crack him and his friends up. Their teacher was a little older and never seemed to hear it, so he'd do it almost every day. He wasn't someone she'd want to be friends with, but he didn't deserve what happened just because the guy couldn't take a joke.

She made it to class just in time thinking to herself, *three and a half more years of this, huh?*

\* \* \*

"I think I want to be homeschooled?" Allie said to Matthew as they ate tacos in the kitchen.

Matthew paused, a little taken aback. "Are there problems at school again?"

She shook her head no. "I just don't want to be there. I don't want to be around such cruel people every day."

"Have you talked with your therapist about this?"

"She thinks if I do it, I need to join things, too. And so I've been researching clubs for homeschoolers."

The school versus homeschool debate had finally come to a head. It's one he no longer knew how to navigate. For so many years, he worried it'd be unhealthy if she were too sheltered. She wasn't that far from adulthood and facing the real world. Would she be properly prepared for it? Would she be equipped to deal with others, especially if they were unpleasant? As an adult she'd have to fix her own problems. Could she? He didn't know, and that scared him.

But he wanted it to be her choice. And her limited high school experience did expose her to some of what the real world would be like. She had faced adversity and rose above it. And she had seen cruelty and understood it existed. These things were no longer foreign to her. But ultimately, being homeschooled would mean not having to go to a place that brought her unhappiness. And so, to his small surprise, he understood and agreed with her choice. Plus, he was really pleased she finally wanted to join things.

"Let's get you homeschooled then."

She smiled a big smile.

"And definitely joining a few things," he said.

She chuckled and nodded. "Okay."

"Woodworking?" he joked.

"No," she said, laughing.

"Backgammon club?"

"Not a thing."

"International spy club?"

"I'm in."

"Good. It's about time we had a super spy in the family."

She got up and gave him a hug. He'd start on the homeschooling process in the morning. Just the start of another new chapter for them.

# CHAPTER 36

As time went by, homeschooling Allie turned out to be a good choice. She joined groups and made some new friendships, nothing as close as her friendship with Becca, which stayed extremely close, but she socialized more and liked these people.

And her confidence seemed to grow. He'd witnessed her occasionally interacting with her photography group, and she fit right in. She didn't look awkward, or uncomfortable, or unsure of herself.

When they discussed it, Allie agreed she felt good in those situations but lamented that she'd revert to 'Ms. Anxiety' in any other social scenario.

He'd told her before and repeated it that she'd gain more overall confidence as she got older. He didn't actually know if that was true. He just hoped it would, and he sort of believed it. Only time would tell, and she, like every individual, was on her own timetable with that kind of development.

She still had a youngish and innocent quality about her, compared to other teens. He'd read copious amounts of stories about how today's thirteen through fifteen-year-olds were like eighteen through twenty-year-olds from when he was that age. So many of them were smoking, drinking and doing drugs already. Allie was not that kid. And so while he worried a little that her youngish, innocent qualities would make transitioning to adulthood and living in the real world on her own more difficult, he preferred the trade-off very much.

He saw a social media post from Cindy recounting how Stephanie screamed that she hated her for not allowing Stephanie to go to some party with her friends where there'd be alcohol. He felt a tiny bit of empathy for Cindy. Raising a teen like Stephanie had to be tough and would probably only get tougher. He also chuckled because he knew Cindy only posted that because so many thought she wasn't the greatest parent for never really disciplining Stephanie.

\*     \*     \*

Being homeschooled was awesome for Allie. She didn't think she'd want to experience any kind of cafeteria ever again. Maybe in a work situation there might be some cliques, but she doubted it'd ever be as bad as high school.

She learned everything she needed in the comfort of her home, saw Becca often enough after school and during summer, and she even made some friends/ acquaintances from the groups she joined, mainly the photography one.

It was clear she had the most experience in that group, and it gave her a great amount of confidence when anyone would come to her for tips and advice on how to shoot something, or how to light, or what lens was best.

She also enjoyed her badminton group, mainly because she talked Becca into joining. They were awful at it, but they found great humor in being so bad. The rest of the group didn't appreciate it as much.

Joining a Spanish group made her think of Monica and her travels to so many Spanish-speaking countries. She was glad they got to know each other and thought she'd probably visit her out in the world someday. But she didn't think she could ever be a non-stop world traveler. Like her dad, she needed a home base.

And she was glad he and Monica still video-chatted occasionally. If she was around, she'd also say hi.

As for her Spanish, she hadn't become fluent, but she was starting to understand when others spoke—as long as they didn't speak too fast. She was proud of the accomplishment and hoped to continue learning several new languages.

*   *   *

A year after Monica left, Matthew finally tried dating again. He went into it with an open mind—and liked several people he met. But for some there wasn't a romantic spark, and for others the romantic interest wasn't mutual—sometimes with him and sometimes with her.

And, of course, none of them were Monica. There was no overcoming that.

After a while, he dated less and less. He'd been single for so long that he'd gotten used to it. But he also still believed in letting life happen, so he wouldn't stop completely.

*   *   *

Her dad dating again had Allie on pins and needles. Each time she hoped it would work out. And it never did. And then her guilt over Monica and him not being together invariably reared its head again. She knew their not being together would always be with her, unless he did find someone new.

Her guilt was something she often talked about with her therapist. It never overwhelmed her but always existed on at least a surface level. Her real parents' suicide was a tough thing to process. She felt she had to be part of their reason for doing something so drastic. The timing of it felt undeniable, as they did it only three days after she was born. And then her father was unfairly left with the cleanup. And raising her, with first her health issues and then her anxiety, had to have added stress to his life. Again, unfair to him.

Even though he never made her feel anything but completely loved, and adamantly expressed that she should never feel guilty, she couldn't escape it.

Her therapist said she may just have to accept that guilt would always be with her to varying degrees. And knowing that, she could prevent it from ever overwhelming her.

\*   \*   \*

Sherry and Matthew stayed as close as ever. They were each other's rock and always would be. And each found so much joy in seeing the other's kids grow up. Her boys were all popular, dating and going to parties. Only Darius considered playing a sport as a career, as he was a pretty good basketball player but probably not good enough for the NBA. He'd have to play overseas, and he was mixed on that. He loved playing, but the idea of being so far away from home was off-putting to him. Sherry thought he'd go for it anyway because he loved playing so much. Her oldest boy, Jordan, was going into sports law. He was razor sharp and honed in on being a lawyer as far back as a junior in high school. And Darrell wasn't entirely sure what he wanted to do but was sort of leaning towards working at Sherry's agency, which was burgeoning. She had a roster of fifteen clients who worked consistently throughout the year. She had to hire several employees to handle the new workload.

Matthew was most pleased that his friendship with Kenny had righted itself. Kenny had found something to scratch his competitive itch—pickleball. The only thing that prevented him from playing nearly every day was when he had to have surgeries from the wear and tear that playing football all those years took on him. But he'd always bounce back.

Kenny played on a competitive team and did well in tournaments, winning several trophies. He also played for fun with Matthew, but not too often because Kenny was too good for him. They'd also meet up at the bar once a week to hang out, and mostly crack jokes and reminisce.

\*   \*   \*

As planned, Allie and her father went to North Carolina the summer after her freshman year. They managed to find a few people who knew her mom, with their descriptions not very comforting: anxious, introverted, prone to depression, mostly friendless.

Allie felt so sad about that because with all their issues being similar, the one huge difference was her parents disowned her, while her own dad chose her. How might her mom's life be different if she had been loved?

At least she had more of a complete picture of her real parents now. Her dad had told her plenty about his brother, her biological father. While not intro-verted or extroverted, he did have friends and a decent childhood. As he became an adult, that's where he dealt with heavy depression.

She definitely inherited many things from them. And she felt awful that they were so distraught about life that they chose to end theirs.

Her life would have been so different if she had grown up with them. The thought of that made her cry because it meant she wouldn't have her father as her father. That mere notion was too much to bear.

North Carolina turned out to be a great trip. After learning what little they could about her mother, the rest of the time they spent shooting photos, especially two rivers, the French Broad and the Great Pee Dee, which her dad promised to capture for his boss.

The headwaters of the French Broad River were located in Transylvania County, which she got a huge kick out of. Her dad, of course, joked that meant they'd see vampires swimming. She made sure her groan lingered. That bad of a joke deserved a linger, she told him while chuckling.

And they chose the Great Pee Dee River solely for the name. Her father said if something had that great of a name, they'd be disrespectful in not honoring it with their photography. Who was she to argue with logic like that?

While there were several boat landings, most of the river appeared to be wild. They delighted in taking close-up shots of herons—and the forests of tupelo, oak and gum trees along the shores.

An exhilarating experience for both. They were very glad they went to North Carolina.

But their favorite father-daughter activity became hiking up and photographing mountains. Being someone born with a lung condition, Allie took so much pride in her ability to handle such a rigorous activity. And Arizona offered up several. Their first, Mt. Lemmon, south of Tucson was 9,000 feet in height and stood as the highest point in the Santa Catalina Mountains. They didn't try going to the top as her dad wanted to ease her into things, but when they made camp, she felt she could climb higher. And it was her first experience walking with crampons, a traction device that looked like triangular metal spikes protruding all the way around.

The next few they climbed were the Mogollon Rim in northern Arizona, Mingus Mountain in north central Arizona in the Prescott National Forest, and Humphreys Peak in the Coconino National Forest, about 11 miles north of Flagstaff, which was the highest they'd climbed. They didn't go to the top at 12,633 feet, but she was determined to one day.

Doing these things with her father was just so special. And during each they reveled in the different sunrises and sunsets. He already loved both, and she had fallen in love with them during their Denmark trip. They decided the sun was their thing.

*   *   *

With his life being fairly routine now, Matthew started living a little through Allie's experiences. Like her getting her driver's license. Thankfully, her mostly play-it-safe, cautious personality helped ease his anxiety about her on the road by herself. But he couldn't believe his little girl could legally drive a car.

To celebrate passing the test, they went shopping for her first car. He wanted something practical, reliable, and not too expensive. After test-driving some, they found one they both liked, a used gray Toyota Corolla. The first few times seeing her drive off by herself was surreal.

Even more surreal was her first date when she was sixteen. It was totally natural for a girl her age to go on a date, but again, this was his little girl. It was hard for him to wrap his head around it.

She didn't go on many dates, but whenever she did, he tried his best not to embarrass her. But he also wanted these boys to know that she was his baby girl and the nice man in front of them was also a protective papa bear. Allie was a good judge of character, though, so the boys were all pretty decent.

None of her dates turned into boyfriends. He wondered if his selectiveness had rubbed off on her.

That was possible, but she was also an independent-minded person who liked her alone time.

Allie's senior year had him a little on edge because he couldn't believe it was here already and that she was almost eighteen. How did the time fly by that fast?

She even had a job lined up after graduation when *Friend of Nature* magazine offered her a part-time staff position. Her work spoke for itself. Phil told him if he could have afforded to hire her, he would have offered, too.

The day that she might move out, while still probably a few years off, was creeping ever closer. That day would not be a fun one for him. But it'd be a proudful one.

\* \* \*

Getting her first car was a moment. As soon as Allie saw the gray Toyota Corolla, she felt that it fit her. It looked safe and comfortable. And didn't stand out in a way that would bring unwanted attention. Once she got used to driving, she liked it and felt proud that she didn't have to rely on her father to take her everywhere. That made her feel like a grownup.

Her biggest teenage moment was her first date. Other than driving, she still felt young in so many ways that she couldn't envision ever dating, even though her peers already were, and doing more than that.

But when Kevin, a boy in her photography group, asked her out, she said, "Yes," then worried that she said it too fast. She never actually thought of Kevin as someone to date, but she felt flattered that he asked and excited to see what it would be like.

Her dad tried not to look surprised when she told him, but she knew he was. He had met Kevin, so that helped.

She and Kevin went to a movie and then had a second date playing miniature golf. It felt more like hanging out with a friend. However, she did experience her first kiss with him. It was odd. Mainly because he felt more like a friend.

She shared her dating experiences with her father, and he'd listen attentively but always had a little smile and head shake as if saying, *How is my little girl kissing a boy?*

Sherry, on the other hand, wanted to hear everything, and reveled in every morsel of detail Allie provided. When she told her about the Kevin kiss, she said, "We have to celebrate," and baked a cake, which cracked Allie up. Talking with her, though, made her deduce it was more of a friend thing. Thankfully, Kevin felt that, too.

Every once in a while, another boy would ask her out, but each time it was for a group outing. And she didn't feel any real spark, and was in no rush. Like father, like daughter, she thought. She definitely had crushes, though. It was just those boys never asked her out, and she wouldn't have asked them out in a million years. Her dad told her she'd get more comfortable with dating in time. Then he would joke that she should wait until she was thirty.

She wondered what would happen if the ones she was most interested in never had an interest in her? Would she settle just to not be alone? She didn't think so. Again, like father, like daughter.

As high school was wrapping up and her eighteenth birthday neared, she knew true adulthood was on the horizon. She had no idea if she was ready. She was offered a job by *Friend of Nature* Magazine, as a part-time staff photographer, which meant real responsibilities. They mostly had an online presence, and her boss, Henry, wanted someone young with a talent for photography to help navigate it.

This was her dream job, getting paid to do what she loved. She hoped it could one day turn into a full-time job.

She wasn't close to moving out but in a few years she figured she might, even though the thought of not living with her father caused anxiety. Not because she was helpless without him, but his being around provided such a feeling of safety.

She thought the first time she heard a loud noise outside wherever she lived would probably drive her to hide in a closet. The thought of that made her laugh as she wondered if someone could call themselves an adult if they hid in a closet whenever they were scared.

She didn't really believe she'd scurry to a closet, but she also didn't know how quickly and comfortably she could adjust to being alone, if at all.

But since getting older was inevitable, she'd find out.

PART 4

# CHAPTER 37

"Happy Birthday!" everyone yelled, as Allie blushed under a 'Happy 18th Birthday!' sign in a private room at her favorite restaurant, Bestia. Amidst birthday balloons and a table with a cake, chips, dip and a punch bowl, Matthew, Sherry, Kenny, Jordan, Darrell and Darius all sang her Happy Birthday. Becca did as well on Allie's phone, which Matthew held.

"Thanks, guys," Allie said as she hugged everyone in the room.

Matthew handed Allie her phone so she could talk with Becca, who had moved to Oregon with her mom several months ago.

He and Sherry moved to the table to eat chips while Allie finished talking with Becca then took selfies with Kenny and his sons under the 'Happy 18th Birthday!' sign.

"How is she eighteen already?" Sherry asked. "Going too fast."

Matthew winced a little and took a seat.

"Still getting those pains?" Sherry asked.

"Yeah," he replied. "You're all young and spry and me and Kenny are breaking down."

Matthew had been having upper neck and spine pains lately and had a CT scan the day before. He figured it was from pickleball, as he had been playing a few times a week for the last few years.

When the pains started, they were minor at first and he scaled back to playing once a week, but now that it was worse, he hadn't played in over a month, hoping it would subside. Since it hadn't, he saw his doctor and got the CT scan.

"Kenny's got four surgeries on you. Gonna start catching up?"

"Hope not," he said, laughing.

"You're fine, you big baby," she teased.

Matthew saw Henry Tisch walk in. He was the editor at *Friend of Nature*, where Allie worked as a part-time photographer. Matthew got up and they shook hands.

"Henry. Glad you could make it," Matthew said, then turned to Sherry to introduce them. "This is the editor who hired Allie."

"She's a talent," Henry said.

"She is indeed," Sherry replied.

Henry and Sherry shook hands. Allie saw him and waved him over. Henry nodded to Matthew and Sherry, then went over to Allie.

Her photography skills filled Matthew with such pride. Someone could gain all the technical skills needed, and she had acquired them all, but a great photographer needed to have a creative eye. And her creative eye was terrific.

She was especially skilled with nature shots but also excelled at shooting structures and people. Her future was bright. He had no concerns she'd ever have trouble finding work. And to know that about your child when they were only eighteen was a huge relief.

"A few magazines wanted to hire her, including mine," Matthew said.

"Impressive," Sherry replied.

"All our kids are getting jobs and might leave us soon," he said.

"Oh, please," Sherry said. "She ain't leaving you anytime soon."

Matthew laughed and said, "We're not as tethered as you keep saying."

Sherry gave him an 'Hm-mm' look.

While he had no concerns about Allie making a future living, he was concerned about her readiness to be an adult on her own. So, he was very sensitive to the notion that they may be too tethered.

They did do a lot together, mainly due to their mutual love of photography, and had never been apart except for when she slept over at Becca's.

But that wasn't his concern. She was still someone who, in so many ways, felt young for her age. That, along with her anxiety and being pretty sensitive might make her transition into adulthood tougher.

She was aware of it, too, asking to do some of the shopping and meal preparation. She'd already done her own laundry since she was twelve, saying she liked the smell. He figured she also felt embarrassed for him to wash her girl's stuff. But more and more lately, she wanted to feel more self-sufficient.

One thing that comforted him and Sherry was their belief that Allie and her boys would stay in each other's lives as adults.

Matthew looked over at Allie eating birthday cake, apparently with a look of deep thought on his face because Sherry started teasing him by saying in sing-songy fashion, "Mr. Overworry."

"Not funny," he said, laughing.

Kenny came over and joined them. "Hers is the only birthday celebration I'd come out for." Then, looking at Matthew, he continued with, "Definitely not for you."

Matthew said to Sherry, "He sent me a text on mine that said 'Happy Birthday. Don't invite me anywhere 'cause I'll say I'm napping even if I'm not.'"

"And he wasn't napping," Sherry said, chuckling.

"Now that you've become a hundred percent boring, I have more in common with Allie," Kenny said.

"'Cause you both go to therapy?" Matthew said, chuckling.

"Therapy goers bond," Kenny said.

He and Kenny were in a pretty good place. Therapy had helped him, although he still had his down moments that could linger. But they hung out more than at any other point since he became Allie's dad. Besides their weekly bar hangout, they watched a bunch of sports at each other's homes. One of the best outcomes of Kenny's therapy was that he enjoyed sports again. He still missed playing football terribly, but talking about it in therapy helped him put the playing part in the past so he was no longer bitter and depressed about it. He even started guesting on a lot of sports podcasts, mostly local ones, to talk about the Cardinals—but occasionally some national ones, too. It was great to have his brother back.

Since Kenny had been through many surgeries, he felt he was a near expert on injuries, injury prevention, injury maintenance, and how to rehab best. They both felt Matthew was probably dealing with a pinched nerve or muscle issue. So, Kenny would tell him exercises to do, muscle relaxants he should try, and send him a list of potential specialists to visit.

Matthew was careful, though. He didn't want to do anything until the CAT scan came back.

\* \* \*

"How is it you got a job before me?" Darius said to Allie.

"You keep going with hard work and effort. I chose bribery," Allie replied, chuckling.

"And the nature route? C'mon Al, you gotta be like your dad was to mine—shoot my incredible athletic exploits."

"Why can't I do both?"

"'Cause I know if it's between me and some turtle, you're picking the turtle."

They both laughed, then he hugged her. "Proud of you, sis."

"Thanks."

So far, her job at *Friend of Nature* was a thrill. She even enjoyed the mundane task of cataloging shots. She loved looking at other people's photos and trying to understand their approach to each shot. She'd ask herself if she'd do anything different. The answer was usually yes, but mainly because she wanted to be original and even take creative chances.

But her favorite part of the job, of course, was getting assigned a project to photograph something. Darius joked about turtles because that was her last assignment. She went to the Verde River, a little over two hours away, to shoot Sonoran mud turtles. She played with many shots, including eye-level ones and close-ups, but her favorites were when she captured their reflections in the water. Her boss, Henry, really complimented her on those. It was in moments like that where she felt almost like an adult.

Her conversations with Jordan, Darius, and Darrell were often about adulthood. They all were chomping at the bit about it more than Allie, and they'd tease their parents about having to let go. Kenny would always joke back, "No problem. I'll help you pack." But Sherry hated the conversation. She'd say each time, "Stop rushing things."

Allie and her dad talked about her becoming as self-sufficient as possible. She asked to prepare some of their meals so she could practice cooking. And she wanted to do more of the shopping to get a sense of what some of her expenses might be one day.

And while the brothers said they were open to living anywhere, much to Sherry's chagrin, Allie wanted to stay in the Phoenix area near her dad. And she was in no rush to move out. Seeing him in pain lately only reinforced that. This was his first health issue that possibly could require surgery. If he needed her help, could she actually be helpful? The idea of failing him made her so nervous.

# CHAPTER 38

"We found a tumor," Dr. Harmon said as Matthew sat in his office, stunned.

The word "tumor" reverberated in his mind. He might have cancer. He wasn't even remotely prepared for this. He'd come in expecting the CAT scan to reveal a bulging disc or pinched nerve and that all he'd need was physical therapy instead of surgery.

Dr. Harmon sensed where Matthew's mind had gone and said, "But it could absolutely be benign. We went ahead and biopsied it."

"When will you know?" Matthew asked, his head still spinning.

"Usually twenty-four to forty-eight hours."

All Matthew could do was exhale deeply. His mind then went to Allie. The thought that he might not be there for her was incomprehensible. And she'd be devastated. What would he even tell her? Should he even tell her? All these thoughts bounced around his brain in a manic fashion.

"You've been a relatively healthy person," Dr. Harmon said reassuringly. "I'd be encouraged by that."

Matthew nodded, not completely comforted by it. Dr. Harmon had been his doctor for the last seventeen years. They were both around the same age, and he always appreciated his thoroughness and patience. He remembered their very first conversation when Matthew detailed how his parents died young and asked if that was something that ran in families.

Dr. Harmon comforted him back then by saying that while certain things were hereditary, lifestyle factors played a bigger part.

Matthew tried to live healthily. Certainly, no one would have described him as a health nut, but he got a regular amount of exercise, kept his weight mostly in check, and didn't overdo things like red meat, alcohol or sweets. He didn't smoke anything or do any drugs. How could this happen to him?

Driving home, Matthew still had no idea what to tell Allie. Since the tumor could be benign, he decided to wait before telling her. If it turned out to be nothing to worry about, he'd be able to tell her that. If it was something bad, he'd have to … he couldn't even finish his thought. Best not to let his mind go there. Only deal with it if he absolutely had to.

Sitting at dinner with Allie and pretending everything was normal was a mental challenge, but he was determined not to reveal anything was amiss. They were eating one of their favorites, spaghetti and meatballs. Somehow it tasted different.

He kept the focus of their conversation entirely on her, which wasn't abnormal for them because his life was routine, and she was experiencing things for the first time. But usually, that dynamic was organic. This time, he knew he was forcing it.

"You don't seem totally present," she said.

"My neck's bugging me a little more. But I'm all right."

Thankfully, he hadn't told her he was getting the CAT scan results today. He remembered thinking when not telling her, "Ah, she doesn't need to know yet, just in case." But he really didn't believe there'd be a 'just in case.'

And he kept reminding himself that it may be benign. The wait to find out, though, would be horrible.

Before Allie could probe more, he said, "I'm going to lie down with a heating pad."

"Do you want me to bring you anything?"

"No, I'll feel better once I get heat on it."

If she was suspicious, she didn't show it. He went to his room and lay down, staring at the ceiling, hoping he could fall asleep until morning. By then he'd be that much closer to finding out the answer.

But he couldn't sleep. It was still too early, and he couldn't turn his mind off. He tried thinking of anything else, but the fact he had a tumor inside him always came back.

He thought about telling Sherry as he knew she'd immediately kick into support mode—and it would make him feel a little less anxious. But again, he figured if it wasn't something to worry about, he shouldn't worry her.

How could he possibly sleep, though? This was going to be a very long night.

# CHAPTER 39

"I'm hoping at some point I can talk my boss into letting me do a northwest theme. That'll be the easiest way for me to visit," Allie said to Becca as they video-chatted from their bedrooms.

It had been six months since Becca moved with her mom to Oregon. They had family there so when Becca's mom was offered a good job opportunity, it was a no-brainer for them to go. But it was tough on Allie to be away from her best friend. They video-chatted several times a week, but she didn't anticipate how not being able to give and get hugs from Becca would feel so incomplete.

Becca felt the same way, but she said the change of scenery had been good for her in other ways. The people at her new school seemed much chiller and welcoming, and more like her. Being offbeat didn't stand out as much. The chillier weather change, though, she admitted, was a not-so-fun adjustment.

"I would love if you could finagle a visit that way."

"Must be a better school if you're using words like finagle."

"My IQ has gone up at least a hundred points," Becca said as they both laughed. "So, how's the secret crush in your creative writing group?"

"Still a secret," Allie said, chuckling.

"Boo."

"If you were here, you could Cyrano de Bergerac me, so I'd know what to say."

"I can still do that. That's why text was invented."

"Cyrano would not approve of modern technology."

"My mission in life is browbeating you into being more bold."

"I wish that could work," Allie sighed. "The other day I had to listen to a know-it-all at a camera shop who didn't actually know it all. He was going on and on about Bokeh shots and how there was only one way to do them, which is wrong. And yet I said nothing."

"Allie, c'mon, you have to correct idiots. Otherwise, they spread their idiocy."

"I know. I just get flustered and stressed and the words don't come to me. Plus, I hate conflict."

"I'm gonna send you every self-help book on being more bold I can find."

"How many are there?"

"Hopefully, hundreds. We gotta get you to speak up. With know-it-all dumb-dumbs and crushes."

"Send away," Allie said, laughing.

"I'm on it. So, what else is going on? How's Mr. Matthew?" That was Becca's playful name for her dad.

"He's got a bad neck. I really hope he doesn't need surgery."

"Oh, man. That would suck. Give him my best."

"Will do."

They talked for another half hour, reminiscing some, before saying bye. Her thoughts went back to Becca telling her to be bold with her creative writing group crush. His name was Theo. He had the most gorgeous eyebrows. She had to force herself to not over-stare. He could probably tell she had a crush because of the way she looked at him. She hoped if he did like her back, he'd make the move, as she knew she never would. But maybe he didn't know she had a crush. Her lack of boldness meant she'd never know. That stung. But on the other hand, not being bold meant there'd be no rejection, because if rejected, how could she ever face him again? She'd have to stop attending group sessions. The idea of that depressed her because she really liked the group.

There were times she wondered if she'd ever have a relationship. The vast majority of people on the planet did meet someone and settled down, but the concept still felt foreign to her. She knew that was one of the areas where she was still young for her age. Just thinking of a marriage, or even a serious relationship, was hard to imagine. And then the thought of having kids and being a mom. That felt a million years away.

She couldn't fret too much about it. If it happened, it happened. At least she'd always have her dad. She laughed as she thought that even he would want her to move out at some point.

# CHAPTER 40

Mid-morning, Matthew came out of the bathroom having just showered. His stomach had that continuous nervous feeling, and he had a headache from lack of sleep. He beelined for his phone by the bedside table in case Dr. Harmon called. He saw he did.

Matthew exhaled deeply and wondered if he'd have answered if he wasn't in the shower—or waited for voicemail? He decided he would have answered.

But he didn't see a voicemail. What did that mean? Would the doctor have left a message if it was good news? That would make sense, but then he couldn't remember if Dr. Harmon had ever left him a voicemail. He didn't think so. He probably didn't like delivering any news over voicemail.

Matthew wasn't ready to call back. He paced back and forth, trying to gather himself.

Finally, after another deep breath, he called. The ringing of the phone felt so long, even though it only rang twice before a receptionist answered. He told her he was calling Dr. Harmon back. She put him on hold. He waited nervously. He was either going to be told he was okay—or not. It was hard to breathe.

As he kept waiting, he saw a 'To Do' list on his desk: 1) Touch up oak tree photos and send to Phil, 2) Look up paint samples for bathroom, 3) Do knee exercises.

All mundane things. So easy to take them for granted. He turned away from the list and waited, completely conscious of each breath.

Dr. Harmon finally came on the line. "It's cancerous, Matthew," he said. "We need to operate."

Matthew was too stunned to listen clearly as Dr. Harmon elaborated. He heard operation timelines and words like radiation therapy, but all he could think about was, "Am I going to die?"

And then he thought of Allie. How would he tell her?

The call with the doctor ended. Matthew sat on his bed. And cried.

# CHAPTER 41

"Painted Hills?" Henry said. "That'd be amazing to see what you'd capture, but unfortunately, we don't have the budget to send you to Oregon."

Allie knew it was a long shot as she sat in Henry's cluttered office. But it was worth asking.

This job was her first experience being in any kind of office, and she got a kick out of the lack of tidiness. *Friend of Nature* magazines were strewn across Henry's desk, on chairs, and in stacks on the floor. A framed cover was on the wall behind him.

"Is there something about Painted Hills that intrigued you?"

"My best friend lives in Oregon, so I was curious about what might be up there. Especially because I'm probably going to visit her at some point. And Painted Hills stood out."

She had researched it thoroughly. It was a site where the mounds and hills looked like an incredible painting with various shades of red, orange, gold, and purple. She pictured in her mind how she'd want to shoot it.

"It definitely stands out. I had a geology class in college where we learned about it. Something about the erosion causing the colors."

"Yeah, the erosion apparently exposed layers of volcanic ash, clay, and other minerals over millions of years."

"Stick with us a while and maybe we'll be able to get you up there."

"I'd love that."

"I've actually put in a grant for Nepal. Pisang Peak. You said you had climbing experience, right?"

"Yeah."

"Good. If we get that, I'd write the story and obviously want you there to take all the photos."

"Oh wow. Little further than Oregon, but amazing."

"I'll keep you posted."

Allie drove back home, feeling encouraged. She never really considered that she could actually go to a place like Nepal, at least so soon. It'd be so far away from home, but could she turn that down? She didn't think she could. The more she thought about it, the more she knew she wouldn't turn it down. She didn't want to get her hopes up too high since she didn't know if grants ever came through. She'd ask her dad about the likelihood of that when she got home.

She also felt enthused that the idea of going to Nepal didn't make her nervous. Maybe it would the night before when reality set in, but the thought of it now gave her a rush. And even if the opportunity didn't materialize, she knew being a photographer would afford her more opportunities like that in the future.

She parked the Corolla on the driveway and went into the house with a hop in her step, excited about telling her dad.

# CHAPTER 42

Matthew lay on the couch in the living room, staring at the ceiling. He had stopped crying and now just felt paralyzed.

He could hear his heart beating, though, faster than usual. Allie would be home soon. There was no way he couldn't tell her. Could he soften it somehow? Tell her that his doctor felt confident that after surgery and the radiation, his cancer would be gone. But that'd be a lie. Dr. Harmon wasn't doom and gloom, but he was honest. He'd wished they'd caught it earlier.

He kept running in his mind repeatedly, "What should I tell her?" It was like his brain couldn't think because he couldn't form the words. It was agonizing.

And then he heard the front door open. Allie was home.

"I'm back!" she yelled.

He didn't move. She walked in and saw him. He sat up, in what felt like slow motion. She had a quizzical look on her face, as if the way he was acting was unusual.

And then his emotions betrayed him before he could speak. He started choking up. She knew something was wrong and rushed over to him. He told her the truth. It was the toughest conversation he'd ever had in his life.

Allie sobbed heavily. Dad mode kicked in as he held her in a tight hug, letting her sob into his chest. Tears streamed down his face. He was helpless to do anything about her pain. This was the toughest moment of her life, too. He'd let her cry, no matter how long it took.

# CHAPTER 43

Allie lay in bed, eyes wide open, unable to sleep. Her body felt so ill. Would she ever be able to sleep again? Her father telling her he had cancer was the worst moment of her life. She had cried for hours. When she finally stopped, she didn't know if she had tears left.

She desperately wanted to block from her mind that she might lose him. But she couldn't. No other thoughts would enter her brain.

But he'd need her. He'd need her to be strong. She must sleep. She must take care of herself, so she'd be in good condition. But how could she turn her mind off from this?

It was so unfair. He was such a good person. How could this be happening?

She started crying again. There was no roadmap for how to handle this.

As her crying finally slowed again, she told herself she'd allow this behavior tonight. She was human after all, and she was devastated. But starting tomorrow, and every day after, she would do everything in her power to help him get through this.

She didn't know how many times she repeated in her mind *I'll be there for him, and he'll get healthy* before she finally fell asleep.

# CHAPTER 44

"I want to be there," Monica said. "I can get a flight tonight."

Matthew lay in a hospital bed. He'd been out of surgery for about six hours but still felt nauseous and weak. "No, I love you for it, but I've got enough support," Matthew said. "Allie's practically sleeping here. And Sherry and Kenny are here a lot."

He sent Allie home a few hours earlier to get some sleep. She'd been by his side almost continuously and was exhausted. She didn't want to go, but he insisted, especially since Sherry was there now.

Sherry sat next to him holding the tablet so he could see Monica.

"Okay. But say the word, and I'm there."

"Will do."

They signed off.

"Allie's going to make herself sick if she keeps trying to stay here," Sherry said.

"She says I'd do it if she were here," he replied.

Knowing it was true, Sherry nodded and said, "I just hope she's getting a real nap in and doesn't rush back."

They sat in silence for a moment. Sherry finally said, "The doctor feels good about the surgery."

"Yeah," he replied. "Still says they wished it was caught a little earlier."

More silence. Matthew started choking up. "You'll be there for her, right?"

"Don't talk like that."

"I know you will, but I still want to hear it."

"Of course I will," she said. "But we're not going there."

He squeezed her hand as she started to cry. He teared up. She tried gathering herself, wiped her eyes, and said, "We've always fixed each other."

He just nodded, acknowledging this time was different. They leaned in for a long hug.

"It's always been even. The fixing," he said.

They stayed in the hug.

"At least I take the lead now," he joked.

Sherry chuckled as they separated.

"You won't let me beat you in air hockey, so I gotta take this," he said.

"As soon as you're better I'm getting my darts rematch. And I'll be the new Bullseye Baby."

They laughed and wiped their eyes.

Allie came back in, and they both said to her at the same time, "Did you nap?"

She nodded yes.

\*   \*   \*

The next few days for Allie were a blur. Her dad was home now, recovering.

That first night, she was so nervous. She no longer had the safety net of being at a hospital full of doctors and nurses.

She checked on him constantly, and when she finally needed to go to bed herself, she did one last check, standing in the doorway of his bedroom, which she kept a little ajar. His bedside clock showed 1:14 am.

She looked in at him sleeping—and waited for several moments nervously, wanting to make sure he was breathing. It took a bit, but she finally saw it. With that, she relaxed a little and walked to her bedroom, hoping to get a few hours of sleep.

Throughout the first few days, seeing him so weak, with barely an appetite, was painful. But even though she was scared beyond belief, he needed her. Whatever it took to help, she'd do.

Henry told her to take all the time she needed, but her dad insisted she keep working so that her mind wouldn't be preoccupied with him the whole time. And he didn't want her to lose the job. She didn't really want to work. She didn't want to do anything but help him heal. But since he was so insistent she agreed, and he was right; it did help her mind. But she couldn't do a lot because she couldn't focus for long stretches. Her thoughts always returned to him, and every photograph she took reminded her of all the times they shot things together.

Adding to her pressure was all the work her dad had to do but couldn't. He tried, but he was just too tired to focus. Allie insisted he stopped trying. She'd do it for him. He needed his rest.

\*     \*     \*

"Will you please go get some sleep?" Sherry said to Allie on the phone as Allie, bleary-eyed, looked at a gallery of hydrangea photos on her father's laptop.

"I will at some point. But my dad's boss needs these pics by morning. I don't think I've ever had this much coffee in me."

"Can't he get someone else to do it?"

"They're short-staffed."

Sherry sighed. "I'll come over early to give you a few hours' break."

"You're not sleeping a lot either, though."

"We'll tag team it, sweetie. Okay?"

"Okay. Love ya'."

"Love ya' back."

She hung up with Sherry and spent the next hour cataloging all her father's hydrangea photos. As tired as she was, seeing the entirety of his shots made her appreciate how talented he was, and kept her alert. The creativity with how he shot everything in a way that was symmetrical was so impressive—and it highlighted the flower's colors even more.

Finishing up everything that Phil needed took her late into the night, so she only got a few hours of sleep before getting up to give her dad his pills. Sherry would be over soon. Then she could get some more sleep.

She had placed all his necessary pills in a weekly pill box because he had so many to take. Reading the side effects on one, she stopped halfway through because it was overwhelming. He had to take the pills, so any side effects were unavoidable. She'd monitor how he was handling them, though. She wrote that information in a daily recap covering everything about his recovery. Any detail, big or small, she figured might be helpful to his doctor.

It hurt her heart watching him take his pills because his throat was so sore from the radiation treatments.

But the toughest thing to watch was when he'd have really hard shivering episodes. Sometimes, he'd be too hot and sometimes too cold, so she had blankets available in case he needed an extra one, and a fan in case that would help.

One night as he tried to sleep, his shivering was so bad she wanted to scream from feeling so helpless. When he finally stopped and fell asleep, she went to her room and sobbed uncontrollably, like she did when he first told her about his cancer.

\* \* \*

"My throat feels like someone took sandpaper to it," Matthew said to Sherry as she sat by his bed.

"If it's working, that's the tradeoff," she said. "I wish you'd eat a little more."

"The tradeoff for that is I'm back down to my college weight."

"Silver linings, I guess."

"Big silver lining. It's almost mankini season. Getting my body nice and thin for it."

"I'm not laughing at that," Sherry said, stifling a laugh.

"I saw enough of a smile to call it a laugh."

"A laugh is not a smile. And at least you're telling jokes again. Bad ones, but I'll take even those."

He managed a chuckle. It was tough to joke around when he felt so awful, but he wanted to at least try to feel like himself some of the time.

The surgery recovery and radiation treatments had been brutal. He was constantly fatigued, with very little appetite, and even though he was exhausted, sleeping was difficult due to being so uncomfortable. Plus, nausea or dizziness would sometimes just pop up out of the blue. He had to keep a small trash can near his bed, and when the nausea hit hard, he'd have to sit up and hover over it until he either vomited or the feeling went away. It happened often.

But he told himself, if it got rid of his cancer, it was all worth it. He just knew it was still an if, and there was nothing anyone could do about it.

He'd just finished his third week of radiation treatment. He had to go five days a week and had one more week to go. The actual sessions didn't hurt, but it was always unnerving as he had to lay on a treatment table while a machine, which the technician called a linear accelerator, shot radiation beams into his upper chest and neck area. He couldn't wait to never again have to hear the dull buzzing sound the machine made.

"Allie's been unbelievable," Sherry said. "Doting nurse, shop, cook, clean, do her job and yours."

"Yeah. It's all so unfair to her, though."

"Indeed. But if there's a silver lining for that, she's being forced to be the adult."

Matthew nodded in agreement. As hard as this ordeal was on Allie, seeing her handle everything with such aplomb was comforting. That gnawing feeling he'd always had, wondering if she could handle being a grownup, was starting to be answered. She'd probably always have her anxiety issues and bouts of low self-esteem, but she didn't need anyone ever to baby her. He hoped he'd get to see her development over many years. If he had to fight for that, he would. With every ounce of every-thing he had.

\*     \*     \*

"All of it," Allie said as her father slowly drank a smoothie, which he clearly didn't enjoy.

She shopped every day, no matter how tired she was, wanting only fresh vegetables in the smoothies she made him. One in the morning and one in the evening.

She tried to mix up what went in each. This one had carrot, kale, avocado, plain nonfat Greek Yogurt, almond butter and some flaxseed.

"It's awful."

"I don't care. It's full of antioxidants."

"There's gotta be a Twinkie version of this."

He finished it, scrunching his face to show his distaste.

"Good," Allie said.

"Do I get a prize?"

"In about an hour you get more delicious vitamins."

"I did a poor job of teaching you what a prize was."

"Yep. How are you feeling?"

He chuckled and said, "Wonderful."

He drank a little water, then looked at her. "I couldn't do this without you."

"Just keep doing it," she replied. "That's all that matters."

He smiled and gave a little salute. She knew how tough the mental side of all this was on him. He was always the one who took care of her. And now he couldn't. On the first day home from the hospital, he had in mind to make them dinner, but it became clear right away he was too weak to do anything. He apologized. She told him he had nothing to apologize for.

Sherry was her lifesaver. She'd cook and bring over meals in Tupperware that could last for days. And she'd stay there so Allie could nap, or shop, or when she had to go to the office or do a photo shoot. When Allie would say, "But aren't you super busy with your own work?" Sherry would reply, "It's good to be the boss. I make my own hours and my office becomes my phone." And when she couldn't be there, she made sure Kenny or one of her boys would be.

And Sherry would try to keep Allie's mind preoccupied. They'd talk about pop culture, tell riddles, detail each other's work—anything that wasn't about her father's health.

"I feel guilty you're doing all this," Allie said as Sherry brought over more Tupperware meals.

"Don't be silly," Sherry replied. "I'd do anything. And cooking actually helps my stress."

"Wish it helped mine."

"Just gotta find your stress reliever."

Sherry put the Tupperware containers in the refrigerator. "That should last a few days."

"Thank you," Allie said.

"You doing okay?" Sherry asked.

"I'm dealing. Knowing you guys are here helps."

"Have you been going to your therapist?"

"Haven't really had time," Allie said.

"Will you think about it?" Sherry asked. "I don't want to have to worry about you, too."

Allie nodded, then started to tear up. Sherry brought her in for a long hug, then said, "When the time's right, we can go back to who you have your eye on."

Allie chuckled a little.

"Your crushes sustain me," Sherry said.

"I wish they sustained me," Allie replied.

"One day," Sherry said as they stayed in the long hug.

She'd occasionally video chat with Becca, too. Becca wished she could be there to help and even offered to come. But Allie said, "No." It was amazing she offered, but Becca was in no position to make a move like that.

"We have this at least," Allie said about their chats. "You help keep me sane."

"Whoever thought I could put that on my resume," Becca joked, making Allie smile.

She also video chatted with Monica. They had stayed in touch periodically before her dad's cancer, but Monica checked in more regularly. They considered each other friends and she still loved hearing Monica's traveling stories.

She was grateful for all the support she was receiving, as Kenny and the boys also checked in regularly with her. And she needed every bit of it.

\*　　\*　　\*

Allie shopped for more vegetables, struggling to keep her eyes open, when her phone rang. It startled her awake as she saw it was Sherry calling. Her thoughts immediately went to something being wrong. Kenny was at the house with her dad, and she and Sherry talked every night at 8 p.m. So why would she be calling now?

With her heart in her throat, Allie answered nervously, "Sherry?"

"Hey, Al," Sherry said. Her voice sounded normal. Allie relaxed but asked, "Everything all right?"

"Yeah," Sherry said. "I'm scheduling things, so I need to know your dad's next doctor update visit first. Kenny said he was sleeping so I couldn't get it from him."

"It's Thursday at 2."

"Got it. Thanks."

"You kinda' scared me, though, 'cause the only time you call is for our daily eight o'clock talk. So, I thought something was wrong."

"Oh, I'm so sorry. I was rushing trying to schedule things and didn't even think about that. I'll text from now on."

Allie sighed. She was glad they talked about it. It was a joke amongst her peers that no one their age liked phone calls. Texting, DMing, or even email were better than getting calls, especially ones out of the blue. But those her dad's age still preferred phone calls. And she was usually okay with the phone, but right now, she needed to expect the call; otherwise her heart might explode. She'd have to tell Kenny that, too.

* * *

The moment arrived when Matthew would get the news about his cancer. It'd either be gone, still the same, or worse.

He sat nervously in Dr. Harmon's office, waiting for him to enter. It felt like déjà vu, as not that long ago he was in this office waiting to hear news about his CAT Scan. And yet, it also seemed a lifetime ago.

That morning, he had made a recording on his phone to tell Allie everything he felt about her. Hopefully, she wouldn't have to listen to it for a very long time. He realized he hadn't backed it up yet, and was about to send it to the cloud when Dr. Harmon finally came in. He gave Matthew a reassuring smile.

"I like how it's looking for now," Dr. Harmon said.

Matthew breathed a huge sigh of relief.

"We'll need to keep a close eye on everything, but today, it's good news."

Matthew left the office and headed down the hall to the waiting room as a swirl of feelings came over him: elation, relief, not wanting to get cocky. In this moment, he would live. He wanted to stay in this moment.

He opened the waiting room door. Allie and Sherry looked at him, their eyes saucer wide. He smiled and nodded. They exhaled with sighs of relief, similar to how he did. Then, the three shared a big hug that lasted at least a minute as he recounted what Dr. Harmon told him. They waited until they got into Sherry's car before the tears of gratitude flowed.

# CHAPTER 45

"Are you always honest with me when I ask how you're feeling?" Sherry asked Matthew as they walked in the hallway of her office.

A few months had passed, yet Matthew didn't feel close to being himself again. But he chuckled and said, "Sure."

"You need to be," Sherry said.

"I think I am, for the most part."

"What does that mean?"

"Sometimes I feel all right, and then ten minutes later I don't feel as good. Hard to explain."

"I'm not just talking physical. Mentally, too."

"Kinda' the same," he said. "It changes. Sometimes I just don't feel like me."

Often, he was still fatigued and didn't have much of an appetite, and he needed to spit a lot. When he did eat, some foods didn't taste the same yet. Sweets he loved, he couldn't stomach now, and periodic night sweats and sometime day sweats would appear when he was just sitting doing nothing. And a feeling of just yuck that sometimes seemed to come out of nowhere.

He often wondered if he'd ever feel like himself again. Dr. Harmon couldn't give him concrete answers about his symptoms because he said every individual responded to treatment differently. He would emphasize the positive by telling Matthew to focus on being cancer-free. But every time he said it, Matthew knew he was leaving off the words, "For now."

Despite not feeling great, he wanted to get back into his regular routine as much as possible. He constantly reminded himself to live for today. Be present in the moment. The future will be the future. It was easier said than done, but the more time passed, the better he got at it.

And he started doing his job again, in smaller doses, but that was also great. It got him outside and doing what he loved.

He and Sherry reached her office's game room.

With her business doing so well, Sherry had hired more employees, which meant she didn't have to grind as hard. She also treated herself and her workers with a game room, complete with pool, ping pong and air hockey tables, plus an arcade-style basketball shooting game. She and Matthew were the ones who used the air hockey table the most. They used to have to go to an arcade to play, and each felt a little silly because the rest of the place was full of teenagers or parents with younger children. Now, they had a place to play in peace.

She motioned to the air hockey table and said, "You ready for me to whup ya'? That'll make you feel like you."

He laughed as they took their respective places on opposite sides of the table. They had restarted their competitions on days he could handle it. But he could tell she didn't give her all at first, and he didn't like that. He felt they either competed or they didn't. So, she relented, and when they did one of their activities, she didn't go easy on him.

They had a good game going and she finally scored—and with the pause in action, that's when he started feeling a little light-headed.

Sherry noticed immediately, "Whoa. You all right?"

"Yeah," he said, taking a deep breath. "Wind hasn't come back all the way yet."

"Let's sit."

They sat in nearby chairs as he continued breathing a little heavily. She patted his back as if saying she's got him, then said, "We gotta make sure your breath is fully back before you get home to Allie."

"Definitely," he agreed.

"I love it," Sherry said. "She's cracking that health whip on ya.'"

"I think she says 'antioxidant' every other word."

Sherry laughed and said, "Our little whip cracker."

Allie was still a superstar for him. She did all the shopping, cleaning and cooking—until he finally said it'd help him if he started doing some of those things again. So, they made a deal. If he truly felt up to doing things, he would. And they stuck to that.

Allie also got back to doing her job. He swelled with pride when Henry emailed him that she was conscientious, reliable and as talented a photographer as he'd ever worked with. He thanked Matthew for whatever role he played in making that happen. Matthew emailed back, *None. It's all her.*

# CHAPTER 46

"Oh my God, this is amazing, Al!" her dad said when she told him how Henry's grant to climb Pisang Peak in Nepal came through and that he officially offered Allie the assignment.

It was an unbelievable opportunity. Yet the moment Henry offered it, her anxiety grabbed her. And the details of the trip didn't ease things. It'd be four weeks, and Henry would be going earlier, so she'd be traveling by herself. When he initially brought up the possibility months ago, she looked up what the travel would be like—and it would not be easy, especially once in Nepal. Experienced travelers had talked about the difficulties, from figuring out the right bus to at one point having to share a jeep, all the while traversing cities sometimes and remote areas others.

She asked Henry if she could get back to him about it. He understood, mainly assuming her hesitation was due to her father's recovery. That was a big part of it, but not all. She chose not to elaborate with him on how she wasn't sure if she could handle it.

Henry said he needed to know soon.

As her father continued to look at her excitedly, Allie said, "Four weeks is a long time."

"Allie, c'mon, you cannot turn this down. Nepal. Going up Pisang Peak. It'd be everything for you."

He could tell she still looked hesitant.

"It'll be the most amazing experience. And that Henry's choosing you. He knows how good you are."

"It's not easy getting there," she said. "And I'll be by myself because Henry has to go a week earlier."

"Allie," he said, admonishing. "We both know the main reason you're hesitant."

She sighed. He put his arms on her shoulders and said, "I can go four weeks without you. It is doable."

"I inherited your worrying gene," she said. "What if I can't experience it the way I should?"

"You do your best. You can't turn this down."

She teared up and he hugged her while saying, "I better get a really good postcard."

That made her laugh a little. He continued, "And maybe a Himalayan snowball. You'll figure out how."

He kissed her head and smiled. She took a moment but smiled back. "I'll go."

They hugged again. The pride on his face was obvious.

She would worry incredibly while gone, but things had normalized to a degree in the last few months with his health. It'd probably take a few more months before he got his strength and stamina back. But he was more like himself, and that was such an amazing relief.

The experience also changed her. She did feel more grown up and mature. However, she also knew she was still an anxious person—and one who still wasn't good at speaking up or standing up for herself in a productive way. Would that ever improve?

Her therapist told her the same thing her father did, that as people got older, they tended to care less about what others thought.

But that's what bothered Allie. She felt she didn't care what others thought about her—yet she was still anxious or wouldn't speak up. That's why it was hard not just to assume that's who she was and would always be. She hated the idea that she might be a pushover her whole life. And could she ever really be a functioning adult by being that way?

\*    \*    \*

Matthew was ecstatic for Allie. And while he'd worry about her getting there and home safely, he believed it'd be a life-changing experience, and she'd benefit from it in every way.

As he watched everything she did to prepare for her trip, a belief developed inside him that the youngish Allie no longer felt like someone too young.

That didn't mean there wouldn't be plenty of challenges, obstacles, and setbacks, but she'd grown into someone who just had a great head on her shoulders. Knowing that gave him such a sense of great pride, but also relief. The thing he'd most hoped for was that she was always going to be all right.

The tough part for both was how they'd never been apart except when she slept over at Becca's. But that was twenty minutes away. Nepal was eight thousand miles away. And then four weeks—that would feel like an eternity.

There was one small aspect, though, that would make his life a little easier. He wouldn't have to fake it around her when he wasn't feeling well. There were days he just felt awful, but he'd do all he could not to show it, which was tough because she was very perceptive. But he pulled it off by forcing himself to appear cheery until he had alone time.

As for her trip, he chose not to give any advice about photographing Pisang Peak. He thought it best that she follow her instincts. His only travel tip was for her to ship her luggage to her destination, allowing her to travel lightly with just a backpack.

Monica did a video chat with them and shared her Nepal insight. She had never climbed Pisang Peak but had been to the country several times, so she had dozens of practical tips. One was taking an international multi-plug adapter and voltage adapter, as there were several different plug point types in Nepal.

Another was not to drink the tap water or even use it to rinse your toothbrush. Most places there, she said, would provide safe drinking water. And he was particularly intrigued by her tip that it was considered good manners to give and receive everything with your right hand—and to avoid using your left hand for eating or passing things.

Allie took all of Monica's insights in, and he could see her appreciation. He liked that they stayed in touch. He felt that as Allie got older, she and Monica would probably become real friends at some point, maybe even travel together. Just another person in Allie's life she could count on. The more of those people the better, especially if things turned bad for him. He hated thinking the worst. But sometimes he couldn't help it. Especially on the days he felt bad.

*　*　*

Allie's departure day arrived. Matthew insisted on going to the airport to see her off, and Sherry and Kenny came too. Their boys would have as well, but they couldn't get away.

As Allie waved before boarding the plane, Matthew smiled with pride and fought back tears. He kept saying in his mind that his little girl was flying halfway around the world. It was real and surreal at the same time. And it'd be a long four weeks.

He'd miss her every minute.

# CHAPTER 47

Moving slowly through the Gongabu Bus Park in Nepal with her backpack on, Allie marveled at the constant bustle of passengers ranging from those her age to locals to monks in red robes.

Vendors selling food aggressively hustled for customers, and she constantly shook her head no as each approached. The food looked and smelled good, which from her research most likely was samosas, pakoras, and local fruits, but she wanted to make sure she got on her bus.

Bus conductors also milled about, announcing destinations, some in English and others in Nepali.

Besides the food aromas, she could also smell incense that she assumed came from nearby temples. Part of her wished she could explore the area more, but she was here to do a job, and Henry awaited at Pisang Peak. She knew, though, that she wanted to return to Nepal one day and experience all the things she couldn't on this trip.

She arrived at the small ticket counter where a long line had formed, which she expected as her research told her getting a ticket could take anywhere from thirty minutes to an hour, depending on how busy the station might be.

Glancing around, she saw a small waiting area edged near the back of the station, with prayer flags nearby. That'd be her only chance to sit and relax before she got on the bus. This was the most she'd ever walked and stood around, and her feet were a little sore.

Finally securing her ticket after forty-five minutes, she went to where her bus would be arriving, double-checking with a conductor that she was in the right place.

She was early but wanted to be one of the first in line to get a seat easily, so she chose against relaxing in the waiting area.

As she stood up front, she felt a packed crowd growing behind her. Looking back, she saw that no one actually lined up. People just formed an unorganized crowd blob. She didn't know how the blob would work boarding the bus, but she was grateful she was at the front.

A tinge of excitement ran over her as her bus, painted in a deep red, began driving toward their area. She marveled at how it was adorned intricately with religious symbols and floral patterns. She wished she had time to take a picture with her Sony A1, but her focus was on boarding smoothly.

The bus stopped in front, ten feet from her and the crowd. Only one door opened. Allie moved for the door—but was suddenly pushed aside. And then pushed back—as if being caught in a huge wave. All she could do was watch helplessly as the most aggressive crowd members made it onto the bus. Only half the crowd got on.

And then the bus doors closed, and it drove off. Allie stood in shock. What just happened?! This was a nightmare.

Even though she knew from the schedules there'd be another bus in twenty to thirty minutes, how could she possibly get on if the same thing happened? She wasn't big enough or strong enough to fight through the blob.

The next bus came in thirty minutes. In front again, she steeled herself for what would happen, determined to ward off any attempt to cast her aside. But she couldn't. Again.

Despondent, she went and sat on the floor near the back of the station and began to quietly cry.

Another bus would be there in an hour, and with the crowd thinned out enough, she'd be able to get on that one. It'd mean she'd be late arriving to Pisang Peak. There was nothing she could do about it.

For the next twenty minutes, she dwelled on her failure. As much as this trip had made her feel like a grown-up, she was still the same Allie. It hurt.

But in her lowest moments, she often thought of her father and his words. He said that everyone had strengths and weaknesses, and too many focused on their weaknesses instead of being proud and grateful for their strengths.

With that ringing in her head, she thought of the strength that led to her being on this trip. Her photography skills. All those who assertively got on the bus probably weren't as good at photography as her.

That made her feel a little better. She wiped her tears and told herself to try and put this moment behind her. Be present for the rest of the trip. Easier said than done, but she was determined to try.

# CHAPTER 48

"You okay?" Kenny said to Matthew over the crowd noise as they sat at a Suns-Knicks basketball game.

Matthew didn't answer right away as he was in the middle of a dizzy spell. After a few moments, it went away, but he still felt shaky. "Not feeling great. Give me a sec."

The sound system was blaring horns and music, and the lights dimmed and then brightened to get the hyped-up crowd even more hyped.

"May be too loud in here for 'ya," Kenny said. "We can bail. Just say the word."

Matthew took a few deep breaths to try and steady himself, but he still felt shaky. He nodded to Kenny that they should go. Kenny nodded back, helped him up, and walked behind him as they climbed the arena stairs.

"I got you, man," Kenny shouted. "If you get dizzy, stop. We'll get there."

Matthew walked slowly and Kenny stayed by him. Once they got outside the arena where it was quiet, Matthew started feeling a little better. Breathing in fresh air helped, too.

"You just weren't ready for a game. Now we know."

"That was probably it. But who knows for sure? I get these little dizzy spells sometimes that can happen anytime."

"What's the doc say?"

"Part of recovery. He says I should test things like this to see."

"Suns were whooping butt. We gotta pick a game where they'll lose badly so it'll be quieter."

Matthew laughed. They drove off, and he continued to feel more like himself. Attempting to do things was important to him because otherwise he'd sit at home alone worrying about Allie. She'd been gone several days now and hadn't been giving too much information about the trip. She hadn't yet reached the Pisang Peak encampment and joined up with Henry. It'd be a relief when she did.

He took her lack of details to possibly mean there were some difficult moments that she didn't want him burdened by. But when you're a worrier, ignorance isn't always bliss.

"Maybe we do a high school game next," Matthew said. "I gotta build up my mental stamina for any kind of big arena."

"I'm down for high school games. Now that my boys aren't playing in 'em anymore, I can relax and enjoy."

Since Matthew was staying away from bars, he and Kenny started watching sports in Kenny's basement more. This had been their first attempt at a live game. He was pretty sure his cancer was a wake-up moment for Kenny. He never used the words "Life is short," but he started behaving more like it was by focusing on the positives and enjoying the moment. He still dealt with his depression from time to time, but he laughed and joked around more and asked Matthew if they could hang out more.

Both regretted not hanging out this way years earlier. They were glad they were now. Matthew loved having his friend all the way back.

# CHAPTER 49

Having arrived in Chame, Nepal by a shared Jeep, Allie waited at a rest area as her fellow passengers relaxed, stretched their legs or got something to eat or drink. It was open-air surrounded by a few shops and tea stalls, and the area was unpaved. Terraced fields seemed to go on for miles until they hit peaks in the distance. It was calm and beautiful. The remoteness made it all feel charming.

One of her fellow Jeep passengers, a friendly man in his 50s named Bikram, sat at a table with Allie as they drank tea. They had been talking about how Allie was running a little behind schedule because of the bus issue.

"I wish I knew you were running late earlier because the faster way to Pisang is renting a motor-cycle in Pokhara, which is about 140 kilometers southwest of here."

"Do lots of people do that?" Allie asked.

"No, 'cause it is more dangerous," Bikram said. "You'd have to go along some scary cliffs. But it is a whole lot faster."

"I'm not really a motorcycle kind of girl," Allie said with a chuckle.

"It's not for everyone," Bikram concurred.

Allie chuckled again. She'd never been on a motorcycle. She was pretty sure she'd never be on a motorcycle. Her being 'Not a motorcycle kind of girl' was an understatement. And then throw in dangerous cliffs. If there was a person who was the exact opposite of her, that'd be who'd choose the motorcycle route.

She still hadn't gotten over the bus station experience. It bothered her. She had every right to get on that bus first, as she was one of the first in line. It wasn't fair, but life wasn't always fair.

But she also knew that so many were dealing with far more unfair things. Like her father. Getting cancer was the most unfair.

Maintaining perspective like that was something she really wanted to achieve whenever she was having a bad day or moment. Unfortunately, she wasn't entirely there because she couldn't shrug off her inability to get on the first two buses.

And she knew she'd have to face the same bus station on the way home. Henry would probably be with her for that, as she assumed they'd be leaving at the same time. She actually never asked. He'd probably help her get on the bus if he were there. And that thought almost bothered her more than not being able to get on it herself. She shouldn't have to rely on anyone to do something like that.

And then she thought, what if Henry didn't leave at the same time? It wasn't like she didn't try last time. She was overpowered and overwhelmed. And she didn't have it in her to be like the one woman who yelled and screamed at people so loudly that she got on, barely.

No, Allie figured it'd just be best to plan on getting on the last bus. As depressing as it was to capitulate, it would be the far less stressful option. She'd just read a book and wait.

\*     \*     \*

"I want to see how crazy you get when she hits the 'no phone service' part of the mountain," Sherry said to Matthew as he sat with her and Kenny in their backyard, watching Darius and Darrel shoot hoops on their refurbished court.

Kenny laughed.

"Give me some credit," Matthew said.

"For what? Lying?" Kenny retorted, then turned to Sherry and said, "And you'd go crazy too if it was one of ours, so I don't know what you're talking smack about."

"Then maybe the better question is, why wouldn't you be going crazy?" Sherry asked him.

"How's it help anything?" Kenny asked back. "Worrying leads to wrinkles. I'm still smooth as a baby's butt."

"Your face has never been that smooth—and you're lying, too," she said. "You'd just hide it better."

"That's the truth," Matthew chimed in.

"Nope," Kenny said. "Let 'em live. I'll leave the wrinkle-getting to you two." He got up and continued, "That's all the wisdom ya'll get for free today." He went inside.

A few moments of silence passed until Sherry said, "You haven't checked your phone since I brought it up. How much is that killing you?"

Matthew laughed while saying, "Shut up."

He waited a moment as she kept her stare on him. He finally looked at his phone. She laughed.

No new message from Allie. He, of course, would be on edge when she climbed the mountain and lost phone service. He'd never not had contact before.

Sherry, as usual, read him well. About this and his health. She told him a few days ago she could tell he wasn't feeling well by the way he was chewing a sandwich. She was right, and it made him chuckle, but he was also curious how his chewing was a tip off because he didn't feel at all he was chewing in any sort of way that was unusual.

"You love your sandwiches," she said. "And you eat them with a certain joy, a certain happy pace, and a gleam in your eye. And you make eating enjoyment noises."

"I never realized you studied my eating so closely."

"I don't. I'm a woman. We see things—especially when they need to be seen."

"I hope I see things with you when you need me to."

"You're actually pretty good at it. Better than Kenny. Or he might see it but pretends not to, so we don't have to talk about it." She laughed afterward, which she only did when complaining about Kenny if they were in a good place.

Them being in a good place made him happy.

*   *   *

"Did your dad give any tech tips?" Henry asked.

"Not really," Allie said. "Mainly confirmed some choices. Like I knew I wanted polarizing and neutral density filters. And when to go wide or telephoto."

Allie and Henry were amongst cohorts at base camp for their expedition. Pisang Peak was behind them, all of its nearly 20,000 majestic feet, and shaped similarly to a pyramid.

"It looks like a postcard," Allie marveled. Surrounded by the vistas of Himalayan peaks, she took in the scenery, tranquility, and crisp clean air with such reverence—and a huge smile. That something this spectacular existed in nature never ceased to amaze her.

She had already taken plenty of photos of the surrounding peaks: Annapurna II, III, and

IV, as well as Gangapurna, all of which she had researched earlier.

Now, she focused on Pisang. The terrain was rugged and flush with alpine vegetation, some she was familiar with, like the many juniper bushes—which were also prevalent on her Arizonan mountain climbs. Other vegetation she hadn't seen up close before, like the forest of red, pink and white rhododendron flowers. All the beauty of the vegetation contrasted against the stark rocky slopes.

Allie and Henry, like the other assembled climbers, checked their equipment. Each had rope and ice axes and had attached crampons to their shoes. All their camera equipment was already in their backpacks.

"Keeping my knees limber is my number one thing," Henry said as he started doing lunges. "I know they'll start barking at some point."

"My knees are usually fine," Allie said as she did toe touches. "Sometimes my ankles ache."

Climbing was an arduous exercise, but she'd done enough of it to know how to prepare physically and mentally. She built her stamina up more than ever before and was ready. Knowing that made it all the more exciting.

They finished packing. The climb would start within half an hour, and they'd been reminded reception would be lost about a mile up. Now was the time to get in their last communications. She texted her father, *We're about to go up!*

He texted back, *Jealous!!* with a smile emoji. Then texted, *Love ya'!*

She texted, *Love ya' back!*

# CHAPTER 50

It'd been six days since Allie had been up Pisang Peak, and for Matthew, being unable to communicate with her was as nerve-wracking as he assumed it would be. He figured this must be like what it used to be for travelers before instant communication. Of course, they didn't know instant alternatives existed. But he figured he'd be impatient to hear updates no matter the era.

He'd watched as many Pisang Peak climbing videos as he could and then would close his eyes and try to imagine what Allie was experiencing. It had similarities to some of their mountain climbs, so he knew she could handle it.

And again, the silver lining for not being able to talk to her was he didn't have to lie to her about his health. He'd been feeling lousy the last week, and he had a few more bouts of dizziness and nausea. Dr. Harmon didn't seem too concerned as long as it didn't start happening a lot. Those were symptoms that were part of his recovery, and Dr. Harmon didn't feel it was necessary to move up his next checkup. Still, Matthew hated it, especially being dizzy because there was such a lack of control.

It hadn't affected his work too much, but he was slightly worried that if it got worse, it'd be difficult to take good photos. Being in nature was always good for his soul, and so his latest assignment of taking super close-ups of dandelions was an enjoyable distraction. Super close-ups required different techniques, such as using an extension tube and close-up filters. Since he didn't always get to use them, it was more challenging to get things right, which helped him stay focused.

Sherry and Kenny kept him more company with Allie gone, with one or the other coming over every day. Today, it was Sherry.

Matthew drank a smoothie as Sherry marveled at Allie's handwritten instructions for his pill and nutrition regimen.

"She hand-writes them all out?" Sherry asked.

"Amazing, huh?"

Ever since he got home from the hospital, Allie had made hand-written notes for his pill and nutrition regimen. She also had spent considerable time finding a smoothie he'd enjoy while still having all the nutrition he needed. When she finally concocted one, that was the smoothie he or she made for him ever since.

"Her penmanship is unbelievable. It's like art."

"I know," he said. "I think maybe she's doing it to show off how good her penmanship is."

"Except for my signature, I don't think I've written anything by hand in ten years."

"Another fine art technology has ruined."

"You are following all these, right?" Sherry asked as she waved Allie's instructions.

"Yes, mom," he said. "One of those pills makes me have to pee too much. And on cue."

Matthew headed to the bathroom, chuckling over Sherry's reaction to Allie's handwriting. He was tickled that he wasn't the only one who found it exceptional.

As he entered the room, another dizzy spell suddenly hit him. This one was more intense, much more, and he could feel himself spinning out of control. He tried holding on tightly to the towel rack, but it provided no relief. And then his world went completely dark.

\* \* \*

As his world came back into focus, Matthew realized he was in a hospital bed. He felt numb as if medicines were being pumped through his veins.

Sherry, Kenny, and Monica sat near, which was confusing. How long had he been out for? It must have been more than a day for Monica to be there. He could also tell by their expressions that things were not good. And mostly, he noticed Allie wasn't there.

"Allie," he said, his voice raspy and weak.

"She's still up that mountain," Kenny said. "Can't reach her yet."

Matthew almost chuckled at the horrible timing. But he had no energy. He was weak. He was sick. And he was heartbroken that she wasn't there.

He looked at the three of them. Monica had difficulty speaking, just giving him a small nod with tears in her eyes.

Sherry's eyes were also watery, and upon closer look, it appeared as if Kenny's were as well.

"So … fill me in. And no sugarcoating," Matthew said.

Sherry started to speak but had trouble. Kenny lovingly rubbed her arm and took over as she fought back tears.

"You fainted two days ago," Kenny said. "And … it's back." His eyes got watery.

He didn't need to say anymore. Matthew's body told the rest of the story. His prognosis was bad.

He thought of Allie again. He needed to see her. That she wasn't there was the most painful thing of all.

But then, in a moment that surprised him, a calmness emerged. And it emerged because he knew she'd get home. He knew he'd see her again. She would make it happen. And he would make it happen. He didn't care how hard he'd have to fight. He'd see his baby girl again.

With his mind clear about that, his next thought moved to himself. First, disbelief. And then a deep sadness. He expected to wallow in that sadness for a good long while. Yet to his surprise, an entirely new feeling began to overwhelm him.

Gratefulness.

And then it wasn't a surprise.

For the last eighteen years, he got to be Allie's father.

No other life for him could have been greater. No other life could have given him more joy. No other life could have been more meaningful.

And while he wished he had so much more time with her, if this was indeed his end, he wouldn't trade with anyone the time he did have with the sweetest, kindest, most wonderful person he'd ever met.

And he believed, without really understanding why, that even if he wasn't here anymore, he'd still be with her. And she'd be with him. And that made him smile.

# CHAPTER 51

Allie, Henry, and a group of other climbers—two 30ish-year-old brothers from Sweden, and a husband and wife from Belgium—had assembled in a makeshift camp. Bundled up from the cold, they drank coffee.

A Nepalese guide named Adesh, a weathered hearty soul in his 40s, spoke, "So, this is as high as I take you. You're free to trek up further—and if you can, I encourage it—because the sights are extraordinary. But you'll be on your own."

Adesh headed into a tent. Henry and Allie sipped their coffee.

"This is as far as I go, too," Henry said. "My knees need a break. You?"

Allie looked up the mountain, smiled, and said, "He said the sights are extraordinary."

"I don't doubt it," Henry said. "I envy your young knees."

She smiled again, full of excitement.

"I'll give your dad a holler when I get down. Let him know you're loving this."

From speaking with Adesh before they started, Allie knew that he'd only be taking them up so far. He'd been to the top himself and felt it was worth it, but for insurance reasons the company that hired him would only allow him to guide them to where they were currently at.

From talking with others and her own research, trekking up to the top, which would be another half day, was not that much more dangerous than what they'd done so far. But she'd be alone if she went now, as the others were going to wait until the next day before they trekked up.

For her to catch her flight home on time, she'd have to go now.

Allie looked up towards the top, which was a little tough to see. She thought about the person she'd been for her eighteen years. While being curious about everything, she had led a cautious life. Never someone who lived on the edge or even close to it. Not with her anxiety. She didn't do roller coasters, she didn't speed when driving, and she didn't put herself in unsafe social situations. Caution was ingrained into her. That girl wouldn't go up to the top of Pisang Peak alone.

But she wanted to go up. It scared her to do it alone, but it also excited her. How disappointed would she be if she gave into fear? She couldn't do that to herself. She was here, with this wonderful opportunity. And she was doing it.

With her heart pounding, she began the climb. Climbing alone felt different because it was so obvious you were alone. No one around to help in case you slipped. No idle chatter when you stopped to rest. She heard each of her footsteps. Heard every wind gust. Every rustle of a bush.

But she climbed with pride. Here she was, a girl born with a lung condition, climbing Pisang Peak all by herself. Something only a handful of people in the world had done. As she put one foot after another on the way up, she couldn't stop smiling. It was exhilarating.

She'd stop every so often to capture photographs of the sparse vegetation, which she recognized as Dwarf juniper and edelweiss. The terrain had become rockier, and the sky above was completely clear, although she could see swirling clouds hovering over the vistas of the nearby Himalayan mountains.

She captured shots looking down, which showcased the differing vegetation zones from lusher forests near the bottom to more sparse areas higher up. She knew she was capturing magic, and it would be even more magical up top.

Through it all, she couldn't stop thinking of her father. She felt so connected to him, as if he were with her. It was as if she could hear his voice remarking on everything being seen in that giddy way he did when he got excited.

It was surreal to her how she felt they were experiencing this together. She reveled in every bit of it.

The sun was just coming up and she could see that the peak was about a quarter of a mile up. With determination and excitement, she put her head down, took a deep breath, and made the trek up.

Propelled by adrenaline, she seemed to gain momentum with each step.

\* \* \*

Matthew slowly woke from what felt like a deep slumber. He instantly remembered his situation because he felt lousy and drugged up. His phone was on his stomach, which is where he told everyone he wanted it because it had his recorded message for Allie.

No one was in the room with him, which was unusual, but then he saw a note at the edge of the bed that said:

*Went to cafeteria. Be back soon. Sherry*

He'd lost all track of time but guessed that he'd been in the hospital a week or so. He was beyond grateful his friends had spent so much time with him. He had moments with each together and separately.

With Sherry, it was long and very emotional. Even though he was exhausted, and his voice was nearly gone, he had been completely attentive as they talked about how much they loved each other and meant to each other. They reminisced about so many of their favorite moments together—and there were a lot. To have a friend like her was the greatest gift. And she again reassured him she'd always be there for Allie, even though he knew.

Kenny also tried to reminisce, but he got choked up and stopped. Both their eyes watered. When Kenny could speak again, he just said, "Thank you for being my brother." Matthew nodded and smiled. Kenny nodded and smiled back. Nothing else needed to be said.

How unbelievably lucky he had been to have them in his life.

And Monica coming back to see him, and being at the hospital, was a pleasant surprise. She had difficulty getting words out, too. For long stretches she had just held his hand and rubbed it with her thumb. They knew they were the love of each other's life. The quote from Alfred Lord Tennyson: *'Tis better to have loved and lost than never to have loved at all* couldn't have been truer for him. But he hoped she'd find love with someone else. She deserved it.

The room felt empty without any of them and he didn't know when they'd return from the cafeteria. Tired as usual, he was about to close his eyes again—when he noticed some sunlight streaming in from a corner window, sneaking past the partially lowered blinds.

He looked at the clock. 5:57 p.m. Then looked back at the window. It was across the room, and he didn't know if he had the strength or energy to get there, but he absolutely wanted to see this sunset. It made him think of Allie. They'd shared so many sunrises and sunsets together.

He sat up a little and reviewed his surroundings, trying to determine the best way to get to the window. He didn't want any help. He'd get there all by himself.

He put his phone in a little pouch in his gown and then managed to sit up and swing his legs over the side of the bed, so he was facing his attached IV. He probably wasn't supposed to unplug himself, but he didn't want a nurse to help. It made him slightly chuckle as he thought to himself, *What are they gonna do—kick me out?*

He unplugged his IV and then stood. He held on to the metal railing of the bed as it took several moments to steady himself. Then he shakily started moving for the window. He couldn't believe how weak he was, and it felt like he was going in slow motion.

After about ten unsteady steps, his legs became too wobbly to sustain his weight and he fell forward, extending his hands to brace the fall. But his chin hit the floor—and blood slowly started drizzling down his chin.

Nothing was stopping him, though.

He grabbed a nearby chair leg, and using what little strength he had, slowly pulled himself up.

Still on unsteady legs, he moved with complete determination to the chair by the window.

Finally getting there, he opened the blinds further to see the sight he wanted—a spectacular sunset. The sun hung low on the horizon, a beautiful orange orb. The sky above looked painted with streaks of lavender and pale violet. Several clouds caught the sun's last rays as they glowed with edges of gold and burgundy, and their shadows radiated a stunning purplish hue.

He leaned back in the chair, taking in its full glory. And then with his phone, he took a picture. And what an amazing picture it was. He'd never captured a more beautiful sunset.

Weak, bleeding, and breathing heavily, he smiled. The beauty of what he was seeing outweighed how he felt physically. There was a pride that arose in him. Like he momentarily beat the cancer.

And then all he could think about was Allie. She was out there in the world, having her greatest experience.

\* \* \*

Allie was a few hundred feet from reaching the top of Pisang Peak. Her legs were cramping, and she was breathing heavily, but being so close she didn't even think about resting, forging upward with full determination. There'd be no stopping her. Through gritted teeth, she ran up, finally reaching the peak.

She dropped to her knees, exhausted but with so much gratification. And then, like magic, she saw the most glorious sunrise emerge. Its golden rays began tenderly painting brushstrokes across the sky, lighting up the clouds and the peak as Allie basked in the glow, feeling the increase in warmth. It was the biggest sun she'd ever seen. She wished she could wrap her arms around it in a hug. Her love of nature soaring as high as the mountain peak itself.

Having caught her breath, she then stood, and with another adrenaline rush, began jumping up and down in celebration. She had done it. This was the greatest moment of her life. And again, it was like her dad was with her.

With glee, she snapped photographs of the sunrise and every angle down the peak. She knew she was capturing extraordinary images.

Once she had taken all her desired photos, Allie sat and just took in the view, basking in the bright sunshine that now made all the surroundings glow. She breathed in the air, fully embracing the silence and serenity. A peace and calmness she had never known.

She stayed until she finally saw others climbing up in the distance. With her soul filled, she headed back down, waving to the fellow climbers as they passed.

About two hours into her descent, in which she had a nonstop smile with every step, she saw Henry in the distance at base camp. He yelled something up at her, but she was too far away to hear it.

Realizing she couldn't hear him, he began moving up the mountain with urgency. Surprised by this, she picked up her own pace.

When Henry got close enough to be heard, he stopped, caught his breath and shouted, "Your dad!"

Allie knew instantly what that meant. Her heart plunged. All that mattered now was getting home.

\*   \*   \*

Matthew was back in his bed and re-attached to the IV. Upon discovering he'd gone to the window, his nurse began slightly admonishing him until seeing the satisfied look on his face. And then she nodded, understanding. She helped him back to his bed, and he lay there with his phone back on his stomach.

And then his phone rang. It was Allie. He answered, saying "Hi," in a barely audible whisper. The reception was bad, but he could make out the words, "I'm coming home, Dad. I'm coming home." Her voice sounded resolute but also quivered with emotion.

"I know," he said. "I'll be here."

They said they loved each other before the reception became too bad, then disconnected.

But it was okay. He smiled and closed his eyes with only one thought. He'd be seeing her again soon.

# CHAPTER 52

Allie stood in front of the bus line in Besisahar, Nepal. The station, set up similarly to the first one she encountered, had another packed-in crowd waiting for a bus.

As she was last time, Allie was in the front row, with the crowd blob behind her. But this time, she couldn't afford to wait until the very last bus. She needed to get on this one. Her heart pounded furiously as she ran through the scenario. She didn't know what she'd do differently. She didn't know what she could do differently. Yelling and screaming at pushy crowd members only worked for some. And those yellers had loud, commanding voices. Allie would never have a voice that boomed. But she knew she had to get on that first bus.

Next to her was a giant of a man, at least six foot seven. She took a quick glance up at him to see he was looking down at her. He clearly scoffed as if saying this 'little girl' had no chance of getting on.

And then she saw a bus driving toward their area. It looked very similar to the very first bus she failed to get on, with its deep red paint and religious symbols and floral patterns. It possibly was the same one.

It stopped in front, ten feet from the crowd. Only one door opened.

The rush of passengers happened again as Allie thrust her way forward. But she got pushed out of the way easily again. As she felt her body being moved, she screamed inside her head, *No!*

She burrowed into the crowd with gritted teeth, wriggling her way forcefully, surprising several so much that they stopped to see what was beneath them.

She kept wriggling and wriggling, ignoring the elbows to her face and the knees to her body. She didn't care that it hurt. No one was stopping her. She fought to the front of the line as the people she passed yelled. She paid them no mind.

And then she broke through!

With full confidence, she put her foot on the bus's first step and climbed up and in.

After handing her ticket to the driver, she turned around, seeing smiles from some women in the back of the crowd as if they were proud of her.

With that, Allie walked to her seat, allowing herself the smallest satisfied smile before regaining complete focus. This was no time to celebrate. She needed to get home.

Allie had tried reaching Sherry for information, but the reception was never good enough. All she knew was what Henry was told by the hospital, that her father was there and his condition was bad.

About an hour into the bus ride, the reception was finally good enough to reach Sherry.

"I need to know everything," Allie insisted.

"About a week ago, he fainted in the bathroom. And I couldn't get in," Sherry said, her voice quivering. "An ambulance came and broke the door, then brought him to the hospital."

"The cancer's back?"

Sherry didn't answer, which was the answer.

"What are they doing for him?" Allie asked.

"Allie…" Sherry stopped and started crying.

Kenny came on the phone. "Allie, get home as fast as you can."

The tears welled in Allie's eyes, and she began to shake. "How much time?"

The phone crackled and that was all she could hear. She stayed on the line until the call disconnected.

Every part of her wanted to cry. But she didn't. All her focus needed to be on figuring out the fastest way home. Crying might slow her down. There'd be time for tears later. She was going home.

\* \* \*

Allie reached Pokhara, where the motorcycle option existed. She confirmed what Bikram had told her: a motorcycle would be much faster.

She chose the motorcycle. It brought her back to when she was seven and fell off her bike, scraping the same knee that got infected in Denmark. Her father had encouraged her not to give up on the bike, but the fall made her feel unsafe. She never rode one again.

Now, she sat on a motorcycle in the parking lot. They said it was called a Royal Enfield, but she didn't know one from another.

It had a single cushioned seat, a large, circular headlight encased in chrome, analog speedometers and odometers, and wire-spoked wheels.

With the helmet in her hands, she took a deep breath as she put it on. There'd be dangerous cliffs, traffic, and riding a vehicle she had no familiarity with. But this was the fastest option. That was all that mattered. She needed to see her father. And she needed him to see her.

She was given a quick tutorial. The starter button was on the right handlebar and the throttle was the twist grip, also on the right handlebar. Twisting it towards her would make the bike go faster. The clutch lever was on the left handlebar, and it had six speeds. First gear was down, and the rest were up. To change gears, she'd need to pull the clutch lever fully, shift gears, and then release the lever gradually while applying throttle. The front brake was controlled by a lever on the right handlebar, and the rear brake was controlled by the right pedal.

So much to remember, yet she was so focused she had it down.

Driving off, she felt the power of the motorcycle as it made a thumping dug-dug sound. Her heart pounded as crisp, cool air pushed against her.

About thirty minutes in, she encountered her first cliff. It was just as harrowing as she thought it would be. Carved into the rugged hillside, the mountain road was narrow as it wound its way along the edge of the cliff. Mist clung to the peaks above. She was told not to look down as all she'd see was a seemingly endless abyss.

During the tutorial, she was instructed to stay focused on the road and tilt slightly with the curves while being careful not to go too fast.

*Stay focused, Allie, stay focused,* she told herself as she reached the first perilous curve. She could barely breathe. She didn't know how long the curve was, but time was of the essence so she couldn't be reckless. *Stay focused, Allie, stay focused.*

Finally, after what felt like at least ten minutes, she saw up ahead where the cliff would clear back to a more regular road.

As she reached it, her adrenaline rushed, and she sped up. Nothing was going to stop her.

The next two cliffs were similar, and she aced those, too. She was now past all the dangerous parts.

She reached a long, empty stretch of a two-lane highway in Nepal, which would lead her to the airport. A spectacular display of colors illuminated the skies, almost creating a path in the sky. As if the lights were saying, "We'll guide you home."

She'd be there soon enough.

# CHAPTER 53

Hanging on was becoming tough for Matthew. His body was exhausted. Breathing became difficult. He had so little left, but he kept saying to himself over and over, "Fight." He had to.

Sherry sat next to him, rarely leaving his room. She'd hold his hand for a while, then she'd go look out the window throughout the day where he could hear her say, "C'mon, baby girl. You can do it." She often even slept there in the chair by the window.

As he looked at her staring out the window, he wished beyond anything that she'd have a wonderful rest of her life. His best friend. Without her, raising Allie would have been exponentially harder. She taught him so much. She was always there for him. She brought endless joy and laughter to his life.

If he could grant a wish for how her life would play out, it'd be for her to see her boys flourish as adults, and then she and Kenny would go on adventures together.

And they'd dance and sing together like when they first met. He believed they'd grow old together and happy, with Kenny hopefully winning his battle over depression, at least as often as he could. That was his greatest competition now, and Matthew was betting on his friend.

He managed a chuckle as he thought they'd both be feisty, funny elders, never holding back. Neither had strong filters now, but at some point, no filters would exist at all.

He wished he could see all that. He'd miss them so much.

His eyes became so heavy. He had to close them. "Fight," he said to himself again. "Just fight."

\*     \*     \*

Allie's flight landed at Phoenix Sky Harbor International Airport at 4:53 pm. She sprinted for the Uber station, exhaustion be damned. Her Uber arrived, driving her to the hospital. All she could think about was hugging him. Holding him. Her life force willing life back into him. If there was a way, she'd find it.

Arriving at the hospital, she sprinted inside. Her father was on the seventh floor, but she had no intention of waiting for an elevator. She found the stairs and ran up.

Emerging from the stairwell door on the seventh floor, she saw Darius. They shared a quick hug.

"Go, go, go," he said urgently. "Room's down where my dad is."

She saw Kenny down the hall outside a room. She ran.

*   *   *

Matthew was barely awake, ready to go, when Sherry spoke in his ear. "She's here."

It gave him a tiny enough jolt to open his eyes.

And then he saw Allie come into his room. She was here. She was really here. He wanted to get up and hug her, but he had no strength.

Allie gave Sherry a quick hug and then came over to him, giving a huge hug as her tears started streaming.

His baby girl. She came home. Their hug lingered for minutes. The adrenaline from seeing her sustained him for those minutes, but he felt it waning. She sensed that, too, and looked at him. He mustered a small smile but was too weak to say anything, pointing to the phone on his stomach.

She took it, saw he made a voice recording, and pressed play, setting the phone back on his stomach.

His recorded voice came on.

"Hey, Al," the recording started. "So here we are... My beautiful little neurotic nugget all grown up. I love you, baby girl. I'm so proud of you."

He put his hand on hers as the recording continued. "I know this is sad. Very, very sad... I'm not getting as long as I hoped, but believe me when I say … I've had the absolute most wonderful life. Because I got to have you in it. I wouldn't trade that with anyone… I got to have you in it."

A tear rolled down his cheek as he managed another smile.

"I remember your first steps. Weebly wobbly Allie. Those little jelly legs bumbling about, trying so hard to make your way over to me."

Allie managed her own small smile.

"And then your first words. Complete gibberish. But I convinced myself you were saying dada… And, of course, who could forget the time you almost peed on me? Oh boy."

She had a small chuckle as the recording continued with, "What was up with that? I had a nice shirt on."

Allie smiled bigger, wiping the tears.

"Seeing you grow up, finding your way, your passions, all your wonderful, weird quirks… Pickles in peanut butter. Why?… But you loved it. And I loved it for you. You've grown into such a smart, brave, incredible, talented person… And a better photographer than me by the time you were twelve."

He rubbed her hand with his thumb.

"Somehow, I believe we'll be with each other again. I don't know how, but believing it provides me comfort."

Her tears streamed harder.

"And I know you've always felt guilt about me. Like you prevented me from living my fullest… But let me take one final time to dissuade you… From the moment you came into my life … you've been my favorite part of every day. Of every day. I got to be your father."

She kissed his hand.

"You're going to go on and have the best life ever… I know you are… You got this… You got this… And that doesn't mean there won't be hard times. There will be. Some really hard. That's part of life… But you got this. Okay?"

She nodded and he rubbed her hand again.

"One final thing. For me. For us… When one of those really hard times do come, and you need some help finding the light again… Just … remember this."

Their song started playing, *"Everything's gonna be all right, Everything's gonna be all right."* They mouthed the words to each other for the entire song.

When it was over, he gave one final little nod and closed his eyes. His final thought—"She was gonna be all right."

And with that, he went in peace.

\* \* \*

Allie could tell he was gone. But she held his hand tight. She wasn't going to let go for a while. Her tears streamed and fell to the floor as she looked at Sherry in the doorway. She nodded for her and the others to come in.

Sherry, Kenny, Monica, and Sherry's kids came in and sat around him. Sherry held his other hand. No one spoke. Tears rolled down everyone's face.

Allie looked at her father's face. He was completely at peace. She loved him. She'd always love him. And she believed like he did, they would be together again one day.

# EPILOGUE

It had been three weeks since her dad passed. Allie had been staying with Sherry and Kenny, but she felt it was time to go home. She was going to keep the house. It was their house. His empty room was painful but also meaningful, because it was his. She never wanted to block any part of him out.

She played his phone recording daily. Hearing his voice helped, but it also inspired her. She would do everything she could to live the best life she could. She would make him proud.

He wanted to be cremated and left no instructions for her about what to do with the ashes. It was her choice. She kept them in an urn so she could look at them whenever she wanted. And she looked at it often. And her only thought every time she did was that the love he had for her, and the love she had for him, could only be summed up with one word.

*Unconditional.*

*Thank you for reading this book. I gave every ounce of my heart and soul in writing it. It would mean so much to me if you left a review, as that will help other readers discover it.*